Claire — Th—
for your
...

SHADOW
ON THE WALL

BOOK ONE OF THE SANDSTORM CHRONICLES

PAVARTI K TYLER

Pavartick Tyr

FIGHITNG MONKEY PRESS

ADVANCED PRAISE FOR
SHADOW ON THE WALL

It has been years since I picked up a book that I could not put down. Part due to my changing interests. Parts due to my time constraints. So when I was liberated by reading Pavarti Tyler's Shadow on the wall, all the elements conspired against me and glued my fingers to her pages and my eyes to her words. The story was riveting the characters took seats next to me on my British Airways flight as they came to life on the page and in my flight. The book is a rest read full of diverse characters and a great storyline. A winner!

Dr. Naif A. Al-Mutawa
Founder and CEO
Teshkeel Media Group

From the moment I read the first sentence, I could not stop until I finished reading. As an Arab Muslim, I found it refreshing to finally have someone sharing my cultural background to not be a "terrorist," but be an actual "hero." The imperfections of his character are what made him believable to me. We are not perfect, no one is, but he took his imperfections & became a hero for the people, instead of a suicide bomber. If anything, I see him as a metaphor for redemption, I am extremely excited to follow these Chronicles. I have always used to say that "Batman" was my favorite superhero, I have no doubt from this point on, my #1 answer will be "The SandStorm."

Mosno Al-Moseeki

I haven't read a book this good in a very long time. Touted as Book 1 of a new series, I sincerely hope there are many more to come. I believe the author has a real passion for the premise of the series. The book takes place in Turkey, highlighting practitioners of Islam and Judaism. Islam is predominant, and the new superhero, Recai, is a devout Muslim. Other Muslims at various stages of religious practice, or non-practice, are depicted as more than flat, stereotypical cartoons.

Java Davis
The Kindle Book Review

Step aside, a new hero rises from the desert.

Gabbo De La Parra

Author Pavarti K. Tyler has risen a "Muslim Superhero" from the sands of the desert. Tyler touches controversial topics which only a woman would dare to brave. The author's style of writing holds a poetic flare in her sentences, which adds to the appeal of the story.

Do be wary readers, as this book is not for the faint at heart and includes scenes of cruel violence against women. For those bold readers, you might want to fasten your reading glasses because you're in for a thrilling ride!

Nely Cab
Author of Creatura

The world needs a Superhero. Especially where people are oppressed. I think Ms. Tyler chose a great setting for her story, a Muslim city also home to Jews, Christians, etc. There are terrible, terrible things that religious zealots do in the name of their god, and it's everywhere in the city of Elih. I loved this aspect of her story because it was wonderful to see a superhero stand up for issues that I hear about on a daily basis. As great as the Joker and Catwoman are, it's nice to see the real bad guys get punched in the gut for a change. If I could, I would send Recai all over the world to fix some of this ridiculousness we let ourselves get talked into. Too bad he's fiction.

Ms. Tyler has found a way to put you in the shoes of each one of her characters, good or bad, and I think it's an astounding piece of writing.

Emily Reese
Author of Second Death

Cover Image by Damon Za
Editing by Jessica Swift Eldridge
Interior Layout by Mallory Rock

Tyler, Pavarti K, 1978 -
Shadow on the Wall: Book One of The Sandstorm Chronicles
ISBN-13 (Paperback Edition) 978-0-9838769-0-8
ISBN-13 (Ebook Edition) 978-0-9838769-1-5

Published by Fighting Monkey Productions

Fighting Monkey Press
PO Box 1278
Landover, MD 20785
admin@fightingmonkeypress.com

www.fightingmonkeypress.com

For the truth-sayers and the trouble-makers who speak the words we can't leave unsaid and take up the battles we can't leave unfought

PART 1

**THE PROPHET (SAAWS) SAID
"WHENEVER A MAN IS ALONE WITH A WOMAN THE DEVIL
MAKES A THIRD."**

*Al-Tirmidhi 3118, narrated Umar ibn al-Khattab, Tirmidhi
transmitted it*

Recai Osman awoke slowly, flickering in and out of consciousness, the sun scorching his bruised and exhausted body.

Where am I?

His foggy mind struggled to remember the last twenty-four hours.

Gritty particles shifted in sympathy as he rolled to his side. Sunlight assaulted his closed lids shooting pain through his head. Sand clung to his long lashes and hair. When the disorientation passed, Recai wiped his eyes with sand-infested hands, only adding to what clung to his fingers, pressing the grains deeper into his dry eyes, abrading them. Recai was covered in particles so fine they filled his shoes and ground into his scalp between each follicle of hair.

Recai pushed his hands into the warm sand, lifting himself to a sitting position to look around. The night before was still a blur. He remembered the bar at Bozoogullari Hotel and sharing a drink with a Kurdish woman who reminded him of his mother. Women who lived in Elih knew better than to be seen in a public bar, but the hotel staff looked the other way; money could buy many freedoms. Her deep-set eyes were so dark they may have genuinely been black. Their mischievous glint and the sound of his mother's language had drawn him in. A thin veil was tight around her hairline; she'd caught his attention with the modern style of having it pulled back and away from her shoulders, allowing him to clearly see the neckline of her dress.

His head spun from last night's drink and a dull throb built within his skull. Recai swallowed, his dry tongue thick from dehydration. Usually a soft bed and a forgiving shower greeted him upon waking. How had he gotten out here, in the middle of nowhere, surrounded by nothing but sand? He hoped the dunes he saw were the ones that resided to the south of the city and not a feature of some farther, larger wasteland.

He didn't remember leaving the bar or traveling anywhere. How much had he drunk? Surely not more than any other night out, but his memory was hazy as he attempted to peer into the past. There were rumors of nomads kidnapping, robbing, and abandoning the bodies of affluent Turks in the desert. But he would remember if he'd been kidnapped, wouldn't he? Instead, all he remembered was drinking bourbon while admiring the curve of the mysterious woman's collarbone peeking seductively above her blouse.

The dunes just outside of Elih, Turkey, were not large. The expanse of emptiness made it easy to become disoriented and lost amongst the shifting terrain. If he'd been lucky, he'd have awoken at night and followed the light of the city toward home. But now, with the sun blazing above him, luck was something he simply didn't have.

Men didn't last long in the dunes without water and supplies. Recai was resourceful; his conscription in the Turkish military had been short but very educational. If he'd had a canteen and some salt tablets he'd be able to survive without food or shelter for a few days. But not like this . . .

He shook his head and streams of sand fell to the ground around him. Negativity wasn't going to help him get home.

Recai blinked back the encroaching fog in his mind. The sun and lack of water already affected his focus, and the temperature was still rising. Recai took off his shoes and socks, knowing that despite the burning sand this terrain was best traversed the way his ancestors had. He needed to feel the earth below him, to listen to the sand as it fell away from his steps.

He undid his belt and jacket and made them into a satchel to carry what few possessions he had. Searching his pockets he found them empty. He was as penniless as a wandering Roma seeking his next fortune. Soon he had his designer button-up shirt tied around his head like a Shik turban, and his worldly possessions hung from his belt over his shoulder.

The scruff of his untrimmed beard protected his face from the sun, and the turban kept him somewhat shaded. Recai

4

took in his surroundings and the placement of the sun and set off in the direction he hoped was north.

Recai walked for what seemed like miles, resisting the instinct to second-guess his direction. The sand moved between his toes but soon he found his footing and his body responded to the landscape as if from some genetic memory. He remembered his father's words from a trip he took to the Oman desert as a child: *Never take your shoes off; the sand will eat away at your feet.* Recai had done it anyway, then and now, feeling more in control with that connection to the ground, its movements speaking to his flesh directly.

His father had always been full of surprises: one moment the strict disciplinarian, the next, he would wake Recai in the middle of the night to see a falling star. Recai had never had the chance to get to know him as an adult. Instead, he lived with the enigmatic memory of a great man lost.

Recai stood in the middle of the desert—every direction would eventually lead to Elih or one of the smaller villages scattered around the city. But who would take in a stranger? A stranger with a Hugo Boss turban and a bruised and bloodied face? In'shallah, he would be delivered to safety.

The sun hung high overhead, beating down so no living thing dared venture into the desert. If Recai had a tarp or blanket, or anything at all, he would have dug himself a hole and conserved his strength until night. Instead, at the crest of the next dune he sat on his bundle to keep his body away from the sand, refusing to allow it to siphon the remaining moisture from his system. He stared out at the expanse of desert before him. Emptiness had never been so tangible to him, nor solitude so deafening.

From his vantage point he saw the crescent shape of the wind-carved dune. Recai's face was wind-burned, his shoulders screamed from the assault of the sun's rays. The city remained out of range; all human life seemed to lie well beyond the line of the horizon.

As he stood, the ground shifted softly beneath him. It reminded Recai of when he'd been a child on his father's yacht. He used to love going out on the water, taking the helm when they reached the open sea. The city of Elih was landlocked. It was the place where his father had made his fortune and helped

5

establish a sophisticated Arab beacon for the rest of the Middle East, a place where Turks and Kurds co-existed peacefully. But, when his family needed to escape from the day to day running of the Osman Corporation, a private jet would fly him and his parents out to Iskandarun where they docked the boat.

Recai walked on with his thoughts. He hadn't been to Iskandarun in years. Not since he'd witnessed his mother jump without warning from the helm of the yacht. Her thin hijab blew in the evening breeze before she leapt. It had been blue and Recai remembered the way it seemed to float in the air when she took that final step. Not long after her suicide his father disappeared, leaving paperwork that named Recai the heir to the multi-billion-dollar empire he ran. Recai had been only eight years old. Since then, Elih had fallen into the hands of Mayor Mahmet Yilmaz and his RTK—Reformation of Turkish Kurdistan—henchmen who were really terrorists who hid behind a thin veil of faith. Recai was sick to his stomach at the way the city was falling apart, devolving into crime and ignorance, but there was nothing he could do. He simply was not his father.

Walking along the crest of the dune, hoping to find a way to the flat area below that didn't involve sliding down the great sand wall, Recai felt a rumble in his chest. A vibration surrounded him, calling to him from the air itself. A deep roar rose from the earth. The pitch rose as the noise intensified, becoming a screaming growl like the djinn's song.

The dunes were collapsing.

Recai ran, hoping to keep ahead of the avalanche. The awesome physics of the phenomenon would have been breathtaking were it not so deadly. Dropping the satchel that held the last remnants of his modern life, Recai scrambled across the crest, unable to get ahead of the avalanche. The dune song reached a crescendo and Recai screamed back at the spectacle of Mother Nature's power. He lost his balance and fell to his hands and knees just as the top of the dune, which swept out from beneath him. He rolled, swimming in the sea of sand that enveloped him then whisked him away.

A hand twitched in the sand before Hasad Sofaer. He looked down at it from his perch atop the camel without much concern, assuming the movement was probably a trick of the mind. Unfortunately, it wasn't unusual to find body parts out here in the dead lands of the dunes, but one never quite got used to it. The RTK had taken to leaving bodies, both alive and dead, to disappear into the sand. No one survived long out here alone. *The RTK*, Hasad spat at the ground, wasting precious moisture to solidify his curse. Once again, the desert's beauty had been defiled by those bastards.

The hand, however, was curious enough to garner the interest of the great beast Hasad rode.

Hasad's camel twitched, cocking its head and lowering its nose to the disembodied hand. The fingers closed around the beast's muzzle, startling the animal and Hasad.

The old man cushed the camel, commanding it to kneel so he could slide from his perch. He stared at the wiggling hand, wondering what kind of devil had animated a dead thing. Was this how the world would end? Was this the day the Golems would rise to avenge their wrongs? Hasad was not a superstitious man, but he had been raised in a tight community of Baghdadi Jews. When the impossible appeared before him, the stories of his youth had more credibility than ever before.

The hand began clawing at the sand, trying to push it away. It twisted, effectively pulling more sand on top of it. The sight pulled Hasad out of his thoughts and spurred him to action. Kneeling down next to the hand, he dug, his camel snorting and spitting behind him as if sensing a rising evil. *This might be a man, a man left to die.* Hasad could not sit back and allow such a thing to happen if he had the power to stop it; God and his own morality demanded action. Too many had died out here already.

Digging along the hand's arm, he found another finger, then another, until he uncovered another complete hand. The fingers reached out, startling Hasad with their strength as they grasped his forearm. Leaning back against his heels, he pulled against the collapsing sand. Hasad strained and his old joints protested until his feet slipped out from under him in one final burst of strength. A gasping man emerged from the sand.

The face looking up at Hasad from the desert grave was sunburnt and bruised. Sand fell away to reveal blood-matted hair and features covered with bruises and scabs.

Hasad lay on his stomach and reached his hand out to the man who was taking ragged, shallow breaths.

"Beyefendi?" Hasad called, crawling toward him, trying to disturb as little sand as possible while getting an upsetting amount down the front of his own shirt.

"Yarmetî," the man whispered before his head slumped forward, his neck gone limp. The stubble of a red beard and a familiar yet utterly foreign language set off alarms within Hasad. The old man knew that for a Kurd to end up out here alone, he was either very dangerous or very stupid.

Cursing under his breath, the old Jew slid away from the man and retrieved a rope from his camel, tying one end to the harness the beast wore. He tied the other end into a noose, which he looped as low as possible around the man's arms. Then he tightened it so his arms came together at an angry angle above the strange man's head. Hasad sighed and shook his head.

Better a dislocated shoulder or two than dying out here alone.

With that, he slapped the camel on the backside and set to pulling Recai Osman out of the sand.

ather…what have you—?"

"Child hush, now help me get him inside…quickly."

Recai Osman drifted in and out of consciousness, voices occasionally penetrating his awareness. When he awoke, for the first moment he was blissfully unaware of the severity of his injuries. He moaned and attempted to speak, sensing the presence of someone near. Scents of cardamom and jasmine drifted around him. *Perhaps this was an oasis, perhaps the desert djinn had saved him...*

"Where did you find him? What happened?" A voice spoke from above. Recai struggled to open his eyes, but could not find the strength.

"Rebekah, this is not the time, he is badly hurt, please...."

The throbbing of Recai's shoulder started slowly, building on itself until the burning pain consumed his reality. Pain radiated throughout his entire body. The serious and superficial injuries all linked together to create a cloud of agony. His mind revolted against being lifted and dragged across the same sandy terrain that he vaguely remembered swallowing him whole. He struggled against the unknown hands restraining him. A sudden lurch threatened to pull him apart, deepening the cutting pain.

Recai released a shaky breath, his chest pounding as if someone had taken a sledgehammer to it, snapping him in two. Darkness claimed him again, leaving his caretakers to carry him into their home without resistance.

Rebekah, I could not leave him out there to die," Hasad explained to his daughter.

His voice was heavy as he slumped at the small wooden table in his kitchen. He'd acted on impulse, allowing notions of right and wrong to dictate his behavior instead of considering the threat his actions had placed upon them. A strange man in his home, now sleeping in his bed! What good could come of this?

"I know, Aba," Rebekah breathed without turning toward her father.

Her attention was focused on the Nogai tea she was preparing for the unexpected guest bleeding in the back room where her father usually slept. The comforting drink was something her mother had always given her as a child when she was sick. It would not heal his wounds, but it would offer him some nourishment and hopefully ease that which was not visibly broken.

She stirred the milk and tea as the mixture slowly rolled to a boil. Setting her wooden spoon down, Rebekah opened the small refrigerator her father had bought from a distant relative. He was always resourceful, able to accomplish things others only dreamt of. Many out here did not have running water, but she lived in a home with electricity and a refrigerator. Retrieving the butter, she closed the door gently before turning to the old man who sat in the same seat he had occupied her entire life.

"Aba, you are a good man. I know you did the right thing, you always do. We will make the best of the challenges God has given us."

"You have too much faith in me my daughter, but I am thankful for it. I do not know what will come of this, but that man…he was dying, an awful death, in a way no one should, no matter their crime. I could not simply leave him."

Hasad feared whoever had left the stranger in the desert; he was afraid of what kind of man he had brought into his home. He was wrapped in so much fear he couldn't devote attention to any of it.

Rebekah stirred the butter slowly into the pot, allowing it to roll off of the spoon as it heated. The consistency thickened, and she lost herself watching the brown tea, white milk and yellow butter swirl together. Her thoughts were interrupted by the sound of her father's chair scraping across the floor.

"I will tend to him; see if we need to find a doctor to come."

With that, Hasad walked out into the small living room, past his daughter's bedroom and to the back room. It should have been storage or an indoor space for his animals, but it had become his when Rebekah reached the age where she needed a space of her own.

Adding in some salt and peppercorns, Rebekah continued to stir the mixture, bringing it back to a boil slowly so the milk did not curdle. She placed some sugar cookies on a plate and used a ladle to scoop the tea into a bowl which she could use to spoon the liquid out of, or soften the cookies in, the way her mother had so many years ago.

Rebekah was not a nurse. In fact, she had no formal education at all, although her father had taught her how to read and do basic arithmetic. Instead, she lived as most girls on the edge of the desert did: sweeping the encroaching sand from her home and helping her mother. But Judith Sofaer had passed away when Rebekah was only five years old, and so the child had been forced to fill the shoes of a much older, much wiser woman.

Never complaining, Rebekah spent most of her days and many nights alone in the small home she shared with her father. Hasad was very liberal in the freedoms he gave his daughter, always bringing her new books – textbooks, language books, even romances. He read very little Turkish himself, only enough to get by but Rebekah was smart, reading books well beyond her age with nothing but an old dictionary and her own curiosity to teach her. Hasad had little interest in the gradually tightening restrictions on women and their education that occurred as Rebekah grew up. He only knew his daughter did not have a mother, and books made her happy.

She had few friends, but many chances to meet new people and even some suitors at the temple. The life of a widower's daughter was demanding, requiring so much more of her than of the other girls whose mothers and sisters shared the burden. Everyone in their village knew Rebekah lived alone with her father, so the women had taught her how to cook and keep house. They had prepared her for life as a wife, the way her mother should have. Her mother's closest friend, Tabitha, had even taken her in when her father left to trade with relatives in India until his return.

Many years ago her father had fallen in love with her mother, Judith, only a few months after making his way to the desert city of Elih. He intended to continue west toward the sea after raising enough money for the journey. Instead, he stopped and made a home with the raven-haired beauty who had captured his heart. Judith was his second wife; his first died in India before he ever imagined coming to Turkey. Judith and Hasad married within a year. They lived a simple life; Judith gave birth to their first child, a son, before their second anniversary.

Ezrah, the joy of his parents, lived just long enough to see his sister, Rebekah, born. An infection the local physician could not identify had sent him to the large hospital in Elih, where the boy received antibiotics but little else, and quickly fell into a lifeless sleep.

Hasad was never as he had been after his son's death. He believed that if he had taken his young family back to India Ezrah would never have gotten ill. The grieving man blamed the hospital, the doctors, the Muslims, the world. Judith never suffered his anger in silence. She would scold him, berate him, shame him, and remind him that their family was an epicenter of love when he sank into depression and looked at the world as a broken place.

Judith believed Ezrah lived on with God: she believed Rebekah deserved both of her parents; she believed Hasad was a good man. Her faith in him brought him back from the brink of self-destructive anger, though a part of him had died along with his son.

Eventually Judith and Hasad conceived again, and his heart thawed as he watched her growing abdomen. He resumed his habit of singing bangla songs to Rebekah at night and even took some pleasure in grooming his camel. The women of the village visited and when Judith's fatigue made it difficult for her to cook and care for Rebekah they took turns helping. A child was a blessing to their world. The close-knit community was accustomed to raising each other's children and caring for their neighbors in illness.

When Judith began to bleed, signaling the end of another beginning, Hasad's burgeoning smile locked into a permanent frown.

He sat in the living room as Tabitha tended to his wife in their bedroom. Rebekah sat on the floor playing with the small dolls he had found for her on one of his rare excursions into the city. Her sweet innocence crushed him as he waited, resigned to the loss of another child.

Tabitha assured Hasad there was there was nothing abnormal about the dark grizzled blood Judith expelled after losing her baby. She insisted Hasad's worrying did nothing but add stress to Judith's sorrow. The best thing he could do for her was continue to provide for his family. Judith did not want a doctor or midwife. Children were lost every day, this one was no different. And with Tabitha's agreement Hasad conceded to allow the child's passing to happen in its own time.

He allowed Judith her grief, and gave the mysterious world of women its due respect.

The next day Hasad left the house to return to the small job he had found caring for the animals of tourists in the desert. When he returned home that night, five-year-old Rebekah sat on the floor next to the couch. She was holding her mother's limp hand. "Mama fell asleep," the little girl told him. "I covered her up, but she's still cold."

Aba?" Rebekah inquired. She approached her father's bent body with a tray in her hands. Her long skirts moved as she walked, shifting the thin layer of sand that could not be evicted from the floor.

"He stirred. He stirred but didn't wake," Hasad said wearily, from his position next to the bed where the man slept. "I wrapped his chest. His ribs are certainly cracked, perhaps broken, but there is little the physician can do. We must watch his breathing though. If a lung should be punctured—"

13

"Aba, we should take him to the hospital," Rebekah stated simply, confident in her every word.

"And tell them what? That we found a man buried alive in the desert?"

Frustration dripped from Hasad's words as the stranger moaned again. Stepping away, Hasad ran a crooked hand through his salty hair.

"I will go to temple, ask the Rabbi if there are any missing men reported from the city. Maybe he will know what to do," Hasad decided.

Rebekah nodded and sat on the floor next to the pallet, smoothly folding her legs under her so the tea was undisturbed.

Smiling, she shook her head. While her father had removed the man's shirt to wrap his ribs, he had not cleaned the man's wounds or swept the sand from his eyes. That, however, was Hasad: always solving the large problems, never seeing the minutiae.

Setting the tray down, Rebekah rose to go to the bathroom. She heard the front door close as her father left without a word to her, as was his way. She wet the soft cloth she saved for washing her face with warm water. Bringing it and a towel, she returned to the stranger.

He lay still as he slept; his color gray. She feared his injuries were worse than the visible wounds. It was a real possibility he might die in her home. Despite the morbid direction of her thoughts, Rebekah could not help but stare at the strong, smooth body before her. The brown skin and defined chest of the stranger made her blush with thoughts of things she didn't yet know. It wasn't the first time she'd seen a man without a shirt; at times when her father would work outside in the hot sun he would remove a layer, but that was rare. However, his wizened frame looked nothing like the man lying before her.

He winced as she washed the side of his face, but did not wake up. She exhaled with relief. The blood wiped away quickly, revealing a deep gash in the side of his head that would likely require stitches. At least the wound was clean now; she did not see anything to indicate infection.

Rebekah folded the cloth to a clean section and wiped his eyes and face free of sand. His nose was strong and Roman, his dark lashes long against his dusky skin. Rebekah could see that once cleaned up, he was quite attractive. The man's hair was black like hers but his beard was red; a rare combination among Arabs.

His face clear of blood and grime, Rebekah went to rinse out her cloth. She rummaged in the small linen closet for the first aid kit she had assembled after her father had fallen from the roof and refused to go to the doctor. She was certain she could stitch up the gash on the man's head with the small needle she kept in there. She would clean the deeper injuries with the witch hazel tonic she had made.

As she walked back into the room, his open eyes stopped her. The green of his irises mesmerized her with their bright color and rarity. What a strange combination of features. Was he a devil from the desert, come to tempt her?

The man sat up, his face contorted in pain with effort, softening Rebekah's heart. Guilt washed through her for her critical thoughts. Despite the pain, he continued the effort until his body was fully upright.

"Shalom," Rebekah greeted him quietly, dropping her eyes to the ground, wishing she had placed a scarf upon her head before coming into the room. She felt naked and exposed. She had been alone with men before, but never with a stranger, and never with one whose mere existence presented a threat.

"Shalom," the man replied. The dryness of his mouth and throat could be heard in the gravel of his voice.

Rebekah did not hesitate as she walked swiftly toward the bed. His face was swollen badly, his lip split, and the gash on the side of his head slowly oozed blood. Ignoring the confusion on the man's face, she spoke.

"You must drink, you have been badly hurt."

"Yes…"

He watched as she settled herself with ease on the ground next to the pallet.

"Here…"

She presented him a bowl with both hands. Holding his gaze with determination, she nodded and held it out a little farther. Rebekah did not help him as he grunted in pain to take the bowl, nor did she smile as he settled back against the pillow and wall in order to drink.

She watched with narrowed eyes as he took small sips from the bowl and grimaced at the taste. When he began taking larger sips, she reached out for him to return it.

"You cannot take too much, you will only get sicker."

"It's awful," he stated flatly, returning the bowl.

"And yet it's the best you have had in days," Rebekah countered with the beginning of a smile.

The man settled back again. His eyes closed for a moment as his body attempted to process the small amount of liquid he had ingested. His fingers moved while he stretched his hands and feet before groaning from the pain in his side.

"Nogai tea," Rebekah stated, rising to her knees, closer to his face. "It will hydrate you and replace the fat you have lost. When you are ready, I have cookies as well. The sugar will help your energy return."

She reached out and wiped the newly sprung blood from his face with a warm cloth.

"Where am I?" he rasped, opening his eyes again.

"Çayustu."

She opened the first aid kit, only setting it on the floor after she had wiped away the sand. Pulling out strips of cloth and a small green bottle, she prepared her tools.

"South?" he asked, his eyebrows reaching for the ceiling.

"Yes, assuming you are from the city, which seems to be the case." Her smile broadened. "You are far from home, especially for walking on your bare feet."

She opened the bottle and the gentle astringent smell filled the room.

"Wasn't by choice," he mumbled, his breathing labored with effort.

"You are still hurt. Your ribs might be broken and you have some terrible cuts." She paused before continuing, "I am going to clean your wounds."

The man closed his eyes and sighed as he slumped back into the mattress. He allowed Rebekah to gently clean the blood from his hair and sterilize his cuts. The witch hazel stung but he did not jerk away, only clenched his jaw and held on to the pain. It was over quickly, and the sizzling sound coming from beneath his skin soon faded away. When she finished, Recai opened his eyes and thanked her.

"What happened to you?" she asked softly.

"I don't know."

"You are with the RTK?"

Her voice was nervous, knowing his answer could put her in danger either way.

"No. I am not."

"Good." *Better to be helping a man of no known character than one who identifies with the devil,* she thought.

"My name is Rebekah. My father, Hasad Sofaer, found you in the desert and brought you here. You are safe for now, but whatever happened to you almost killed you."

Rebekah's voice did not tremble, despite her frayed nerves. She trusted in her father as much as she trusted in God. She knew whatever brought this man here was in His plan, and she would play her role with strength and dignity. And so, the diminutive woman held Recai's gaze.

"I—"

"Shush, there is no need to say anything. You will tell me everything soon enough. For now, I can get you some bourbon to drink if you'd like—to help with the pain. I'm going to have to give you some stitches."

"I don't drink."

"Ahh…a Muslim!"

Recai met her eyes to find them sparkling.

"A Jew," he felt his lips widen in return.

"Assalaamu alaykum," Rebekah bowed her head in greeting.

"Shalom Rebekah, I am Recai."

"Well Recai, your prophet may not want you to drink, but I doubt he wanted you to suffer stitches without medicine. If I can find an Aspirin, will you concede to take that?"

Her soft voice soothed her slight mocking tone, making it playful and kind.

"I have suffered worse than stitches without help, I can bear it again."

Recai turned his head to the wall and grimaced as Rebekah's embroidery needle pierced his scalp.

Hasad Sofaer hadn't wanted to take the man sleeping in his back room to the hospital or to the doctor. In all honesty, he didn't want him in the house. Were Hasad a different man, he would have put him on the bus that came through their small town every three days, paid the fare, and let the stranger be someone else's problem. But he'd seen too much death in his time——thanks to the RTK. He had seen too many men disappear from their homes and known too many women harassed by the morality police. He did not believe this man had necessarily done anything wrong.

In these times, the criminals are the law and the heroes are the ones running the dangerous underground.

Seeking the advice of the Rabbi had calmed Hasad's nerves. The Rabbi assured him the man had come into his care and keeping by God's plan. Arriving home, his confidence was confirmed when he found his daughter humming, her hair neatly contained under one of her few head scarves, cooking lentils and minced meat with rice.

Hasad walked past her directly into the back room, where the stranger slept. His face—now smooth instead of gripped by pain—appeared years younger despite the scars, now that he was clean. Hasad relaxed as he took in the man's returned color, no longer sickly jaundiced.

"Rebekah," the old man greeted his daughter as he returned to the small kitchen.

He sat at the table so as to stay out of her way. She spun to greet him, and with her hair pulled back in the makeshift hijab, Hasad saw the beautiful woman she had become. Her mother's unblemished olive skin shone beneath the pink scarf; the contrast in color complemented her beauty. Just like Judith she stood with both feet firmly planted on the ground when she spoke, never raising her voice but never backing down from something she believed in. Rebekah had turned seventeen last month, old enough for a family and a home of her own.

It is time for her to marry. Keeping her here is selfish.

Hasad massaged his swollen joints in his hands, feeling his age in their ache.

"Aba, the man woke while you were gone," she said over the lentils sizzling on the stove top.

Hasad nodded and asked, "Did he speak?"

"Yes, Aba."

Hasad stood with a determined face and strode back toward the living room.

"No, let him sleep." Rebekah followed. "I don't believe he is a danger to us. He was awake only for a few moments, but he spoke clearly and seemed to have a level head."

Hasad nodded. For some reason, this did not surprise him.

"His name is Recai."

"A Kurd," Hasad confirmed, returning to the kitchen and retaking his place at the table.

"Yes, and he was kind about being helped by Jews."

"Damn. It would be easier to put him out if he'd been a bigot."

The old man slumped into his rickety chair. Religious persecution rarely reached Çayustu; they were a small and insular community. But if the wrong person was crossed, or helped . . .

"He doesn't remember what happened, Aba." Rebekah sat across from her father, placing her spatula on a plate. "He allowed me to clean his wounds and stitch the gash on his head, then he thanked me and fell back asleep."

"Did he mention . . . is he with . . . ?"

"I asked if he was RTK," the girl admitted.

"Rebekah! You know how dangerous—"

"I know. I do, but he was so easy to talk to—I had to know. Aba, he says he's not. I believe him."

Hasad shook his head and smiled at his daughter. Her instincts about people were keen and he trusted her. Given the choice he'd rather believe in her than submit to suspicion and fear.

Words drifted out to Recai but he couldn't take meaning from them; the sounds lined up in a row in his mind but they made no sense. The voices were hushed and familiar. His mouth was dry and his tongue thick, but as he leaned to reach the tea Rebekah had left him a sharp pain cut through his side. He gasped and pulled his arm back. Leaning back into the bed, he sighed. The heavy ache of his face and the sting of his cuts were nothing compared to the agony of his broken ribs.

He needed to get home. He needed to get to somewhere with a phone so he could call his housekeeper and have her send someone to pick him up. He needed to see a physician.

At least I'm safe for now.

The old man could have easily left him in the desert to die, and the kindness of the woman who tended him spoke to their character. Why would they rescue him and take such a risk only to hurt him now? No, naïve or not, Recai chose to believe there was still good in some people.

At least whoever had done this to him could not find him here.

Çayustu, he lamented. *Not even a real town. Are there any paved roads that even come out this far?*

He was no farther from home than if he had gone to Diyabakir to attend one of the achingly boring meetings the Board of Directors insisted he attend periodically. Keeping up appearances and maintaining the reputation of the Osman Corporation was his only job, and he felt ill every time he sat beneath his father's portrait. The only reason he didn't turn his back on the whole thing and move overseas was the nagging need to honor his mother's memory.

This little village was a blip on the map, could barely even be considered a town. Recai had never been here before—no reason to come this far—but he'd heard of it and knew that some of his friends had come out here to meet tour guides for trips into the desert. No, given the circumstances he was farther than an hour and a half from the city. Here he had nothing but his feet and a maybe a camel.

Recai wiggled his toes and pulled up the sheet covering him, revealing his bandaged feet.

"Probably second degree burns," Hasad said as he walked into the small room, his daughter following behind with something that smelled delicious.

"Easier to navigate without shoes," Recai replied, slowly hoisting himself up. Pain shot through him but he bit back a groan. He took in the appearance of the old man who'd saved him from certain death.

Hasad's pursed face was hardened by age and a life spent in the sun. His dark skin betrayed his Indian heritage, making him an anomaly in Turkey. Recai could still remember when the enclaves of Bangladeshi Jews who had lived in Elih had mostly evacuated, when Mayor Yilmaz declared the return of Shariah law and the absolute power of the RTK.

"Stupid without shoes," the man retorted with a snort as he uncrossed his arms and stepped closer to the interloper. "We will have dinner here with you, then tomorrow I will go to the next village and find a phone. You have money for a taxi?"

"At home, that will be no problem. Thank you for your hospitality."

The old man snorted again. "Hospitality has nothing to do with it. I find a man dying, I cannot leave him. I'm glad you are healing quickly, but it will be days before you can walk on those feet, maybe weeks before you can go without your ribs being bandaged."

"I will have a physician look at me when I get home. I am sure your care has been exemplary."

Recai smiled at Rebekah who blushed and handed him a plate.

"Bazlama with minced meat," she said before passing him a cup of water. She sat on the floor and served herself and her father the same meal with beer.

"A good beer cleanses a man's soul." The man took a long

drink and smiled. "My name is Hasad Sofaer. You met my daughter, Rebekah."

"Yes, she has been very kind."

Recai looked over at the girl and noticed she had pulled her hair up under a veil, probably for his benefit, as was fitting. He was touched by her show of respect as well as by the gentle features of her face. She was nothing like the women he was used to—silly and immature. Instead, a simple honesty radiated from her.

The three sat and ate in silence, pausing only to drink. Recai ate slowly to avoid upsetting his system, but found the food so delicious that it was difficult to refrain from taking huge mouthfuls and gulping it down. When Hasad finished eating, he drained his beer and looked directly at the injured man occupying his bed.

"Now you're fed. You've been stitched up and the color is returning to your face. Now, you can tell us who you are."

"My name is Recai. I come from Elih. I was born there but left to travel. I only came back home because my father's business is in need of new . . . oversight."

Without telling them who he actually was, Recai recited some of his history. He did not lie, did not tell any untruths, but he did leave out that he was an Osman, the only son of Baris and Pinar Osman. To volunteer his family name would open him up to demands for ransom and other troubles. These people seemed good, but it was impossible to know what someone was capable of when real power was placed in their hands.

"Recai, you are Kurdish," Hasad stated.

"In part."

"You spoke Kurdish in the desert, but your accent is strange."

Hasad had intended it as a question, but he spoke plainly.

"My mother was Kurdish, my father native to Elih. I received most of my schooling overseas in England. So yes, my accent has many influences."

Hasad considered this information for a moment before continuing with his investigation.

"You are Muslim."

"Yes."

"Rebekah says you don't drink. Do you follow all the tenants of your religion?"

"No, I do not," Recai confided, once again taking the risk of believing that these people were not associated with the RTK. "In fact, I do drink, but from what little I remember, that is what led me to whatever my current predicament is. So for now, I would like to keep my mind as clear as possible."

Hasad peered at Recai before clapping once, and breaking out into a hearty laugh.

"Yes well, we cannot all be as pious as some would like. Even the Pope has to wipe his ass with his right hand from time to time. Now, Bey Recai, you should rest." Hasad said, using the prefix 'Bey' as a sign of respect.

With that Hasad stood and left the small room, taking his dishes as well as Recai's with him, unlike most men, who would have left those things for Rebekah to do. Recai had stumbled upon some very good people indeed. Rebekah remained at his side, her food half eaten, studying the lines of the blanket covering Recai's legs.

"Thank you, Rebekah," he whispered, looking over at her and suddenly aware that Hasad had left them unsupervised.

Recai wasn't a conservative man; he'd dated many women and had known more than a few in ways frowned upon by his culture. But Rebekah interested him. Her quick wit reminded him of the women he had met in university in Britain, but there was more to her than that. Something that spoke of home.

When he was younger, he had found Western women exciting. A woman with a mind of intellect and a body for exploring things forbidden to him in the religious community he grew up in had been new and intoxicating. Soon he learned that while their minds stimulated him, their Western ways quickly wore on his nerves, always displaying themselves and jockeying for attention. Rebekah seemed like a woman to spar words with, and to respect. She was a novelty in the oppressed culture of Elih.

"You are very welcome, Recai." The corners of her mouth moved up as she spoke, her smile belying her demure stance. "My father likes you."

"Does he?"

Recai allowed himself to sink lower into the mattress, fatigue returning to him now that he had been fed.

"Yes, he values honesty. Remember that and you may have found an ally in him."

Her eyes lingered on his, open and honest. Rebekah's ease and confidence impressed him. After his ordeal, he couldn't help but consider the importance of having someone on your side.

With that thought paramount in his mind, Recai Osman drifted off to sleep.

Morning came early in the small house on the edge of the desert. One injured Muslim didn't mean the world stopped turning, and Hasad had things to do. There were animals to care for and the day's food to prepare. His morning chores didn't take long, with only the one camel and a few other livestock to feed, but the work needed to be done. This life was nothing like the one he had dreamed of in India; this life he would abandon if not for his beautiful daughter.

Before the sun rose, Rebekah was up boiling vegetables and spicing a sauce for his lunch—food she wrapped easily in paper and that he could eat with his hands. He would be gone most of the day, trading and looking for a day's work where he could find it. Plus today he had the task of finding a ride for Recai back to the city.

Hasad contemplated the man sleeping in the back room of his home. He was nothing like any other Muslim he had met before. There had been no judgment of their home, their religion, or of his daughter's outspoken nature. To have Rebekah relegated to living in fear and covering her body thanks to the requirements of another man's religion outraged Hasad. Seeing someone from outside his community regard her as a person, a wonderful person at that, was refreshing.

As he readied to leave the house, Hasad kissed Rebekah and squeezed her tighter than usual.

"Child, the gun is under the couch."

"Aba—" she protested, but he held his hand up.

"Recai seems a good man, but if he is not you aren't to hesitate. And if anyone comes to the door..."

"I know, Aba. I close the door to the back and put on my burqa. I know, I am alone almost every day."

"Yes, but today, there is actually more to fear."

Hasad hesitated, reconsidering his decision to leave her alone with Recai. But he dismissed the thought. Besides earning a living, he had to arrange for the man's departure if he was ever to be rid of him.

Hasad walked out of the house without another word to his daughter and without checking on Recai. He wasn't dead; Hasad could hear his rattled breathing. *God help me if there's fluid in his lungs.* Was he saving a life or harboring a wanted criminal? Either way, it was time for Recai to go.

Outside, the air was dry, and the familiar taste of the desert greeted Hasad. He had lived here for so long it was hard to imagine his life before. Sand disguised the lines separating road from yard, deep tire tracks and packed-down earth the only marks distinguishing between the two. The few houses near him were bustling with activity: boys heading off to school or work, men congregating to pass the time, women and infants beginning their routine within the home.

Homes in Çayustu were old and in poor repair. It wasn't unusual to see an entire wall replaced with a lean-to or a window without screens. Chickens clucked as they scurried from yard to yard, having escaped one of the make-shift pens so many people had. Hasad could smell spices swirling in the air from kitchens where the day's cooking had begun. Cardamom and cumin, and the taste of yeast accented his hunger.

In a time past, he had been a wealthy man, an engineer teaching at Mumbai University. In a time past, he had a lovely young wife and two small children. In a time past, he did not fear those in charge. It was so long ago it was hard to believe that he was that same man. Now he was poor. A trader. A member of the slave underclass who worked wherever necessary to provide his daughter with as good a life as he could.

Yes, it was time for her to marry; perhaps to a man who could offer her a life like the one Hasad had fled.

R ecai woke slowly. As the aches and pains of his body demanded recognition, his mind was overrun with the memories of the last thirty-six hours. He recalled meeting the mysterious woman with his mother's accent. The desert. Almost certain death. And now being here, in Rebekah's expert care.

Groaning once again, he sat up and appraised his surroundings with a fresh clarity of mind. His "bedroom" was actually a converted storage room, full of animal feed and blankets. Stockpiled food lay stacked on shelves: dried fruits, bags of nuts, jarred jelly and chutney. The room was built to serve as a porch, connected to the rest of the home but not built with nearly the attention to detail and quality as the rest. But he was safe, and dry, and the bed was kind. Despite his penchant for luxury, he decided this Jewish family's display of human decency made this among the best places he'd ever stayed.

Recai found sitting up to be easier, and decided to get to his feet. Determined to move around and care for himself, Recai gritted his teeth as he prepared for the inevitable pain. Dressed in cotton pants presumably belonging to Hasad, he stood. An avalanche of agony crashed over him. With a thud, Recai fell solidly to the ground. He cried out from the sudden ripping in his knee as the injured joint bent more than it should have. His damaged feet, ribs, and left knee throbbed.

"Recai!" Rebekah called from the kitchen, running in to investigate what had caused her patient to cry out. "What have you done?! Why didn't you call me?"

She looked him over to make sure none of his healing wounds had re-opened from the fall.

"I'm fine," he smiled through clenched teeth. "I only bent my knee too far, but look—I can straighten it!"

He moved to extend his leg but grimaced as he forced the angle.

"Don't hurt yourself worse in the name of pride," she teased. "I'm sure that in other circumstances your leg can bend and straighten quite impressively."

Her smile was radiant. Wavy black hair whispered around the frame of her face, unwilling to be completely tamed by her headscarf. The consideration she showed in covering within her own home touched him. It wasn't necessary—he was a guest—but he appreciated her gesture.

The two struggled together to get Recai back into the bed, where he succumbed to the weakness of his body. It had taken three tries and much more contact between the two than should have been allowed to manage it. But in the end, both were laughing comfortably, although Recai's voice was ragged and his breathing labored. As she gently tucked him in, she chuckled beneath her breath.

"It's not nice to laugh at an infirm man," Recai feigned offense.

She laughed openly.

"It's not nice to show up on a woman's doorstep bloody and missing pieces of yourself!"

"Not the best first impression I admit."

He scooted against the wall to make room for her to sit. She sat gingerly on the edge of his bed, careful not to allow their bodies to touch.

"No, but it is the most memorable."

"Memorable I will take."

Recai's tone was soft and sincere; his face relaxed into a grin.

"Are you hungry?" Rebekah asked.

"Yes, thank you."

She stood and patted down her skirt. Rebekah left and quickly returned holding two bowls of oatmeal with raisins and dried apricots.

"I didn't add anything to it. Do you want sugar or cinnamon?"

27

"No, this is wonderful."

Recai took the proffered bowl and blew on the steaming meal. He shifted on his bed, hoping she would join him again. But Rebekah lowered herself to the floor, her skirt pooling around her legs.

"Are you feeling better? Your color has improved."

"Yes, much. I don't feel like I'm actually being processed through a meat grinder."

He sat up straighter, away from the wall and began eating. The thick oatmeal warmed him within.

"I can fix that. I have one in the kitchen."

Rebekah's tone was flat as she cocked her head and looked at him with mock sincerity. Recai barked a laugh.

"Such a generous offer, but no, I'll pass for now."

"If you're sure."

She shrugged her shoulders and began her meal.

Silence surrounded them as they ate. Rebekah's eyes remained on the floor or her food, for the most part, but now and then Recai would catch her peering up at him. She was a curiosity. Living out here at the edge of civilization was a woman with intelligence and humor. She was more interesting than most of the men he encountered in Elih, but was graced with a soft beauty. This world had beaten the individuality out of most people and here, where chickens strolled casually in the street, was a woman of worth.

The day passed slowly, with Recai napping on and off. Rebekah went about her day as usual, dusting the thin film of sand that covered every surface in her home and then sweeping it all outside, only to have the wind blow it back in through the cracks around the doors and windows. Sometimes she would hum softly to herself, and Recai would close his eyes, pretending to be asleep so she would continue.

She prepared lunch and they ate together again, laughing more easily, becoming comfortable with the strangeness of their burgeoning friendship.

Recai still found it difficult to move, His badly blistering feet required Rebekah to change the dressings often. His vulnerability embarrassed him but Rebekah tended to him quickly and without fuss. She simply did what needed to be done and moved on to her next task, her smile quick to return whenever she glanced his way. A sharp knock at the door broke their peaceful afternoon.

Knock. Just one solid sound.

Recai sat up too quickly and fell back against his mattress gasping as Rebekah stuck her head into his small room, her face creased with worry and fear.

"Cover yourself and stay silent," she whispered before closing the door and rushing back into the living room to retrieve her burqa and open the door. Recai heard the movement of the heavy fabric she wore on top of her house dress as she moved across the room to greet their visitor. He wondered if she had retrieved her father's gun which he'd overheard Hasad say was under the couch in the living room.

Before hiding beneath the thin sheet that covered him, he reached down and pulled the rug from the floor and threw it across his legs. He covered his head and melted against the wall with the pillow on top of his upper body. Feeling foolish, Recai laid there, wishing he had his ID, his phone, anything to help bribe his way out of this situation if it was indeed the RTK at the door.

Perhaps it's just a neighbor, he thought. *A neighbor come to ask after Rebekah's father's health or to borrow some salt.* His attempt at rationalizing the unexpected visit did not quell his fears. The RTK made a habit of performing home inspections, especially if they suspected a woman alone. It wasn't a safe time for anyone under the jurisdiction of Mayor Yilmaz.

Rebekah's voice from the front room was soft and gentle. Recai could not make out the words but he managed to hear the sound of another voice. Was it a man? What man would she let into her home, knowing he was back here and her father away? Only one she could not turn away. Recai squeezed his eyes shut and prayed to Allah that it was her Rabbi, come to check on her.

" . . . Only a storeroom, my father sleeps back here with the supplies and sometimes the animals so I can have the proper privacy a woman should be afforded," Recai heard her say.

Rebekah's voice was right outside the door to his room. She remained calm, not a hint of fear betrayed her. Few were able to handle themselves as coolly as she sounded. Recai prayed her strength would be enough.

They were in trouble. The only men who would feel at liberty to explore a woman's home when she was alone were the RTK and their morality police. No one else possessed the sheer hypocritical audacity. And to come all the way out here, to this nothing village without even a paved road or proper mosque. Recai had the fleeting thought that perhaps this was not about Rebekah but about him and however he had ended up in the desert on the brink of death.

The door swung open abruptly, startling Recai despite his knowing it would happen. He was as covered as was feasible. He willed himself to fade into the shadows of the small room and tried not to breathe. *In'shallah* this would all be over soon.

"If you wish to see the extra food for the animals and what preserves I was able to can last year, you are more than welcome to it," Rebekah said with a touch more attitude than was prudent.

Recai heard a heavy pair of feet walk to the center of the room. The intruder smelled like sun-burnt leather and breathed loudly. His boots scraped on the concrete floor as he took a cursory look at the room.

"There's nothing back here," he called to the main room in Turkish. But another voice responded quickly, coming closer.

"There's something not right with the bathroom. There is blood on a towel and a first aid kit is set out. Has someone been hurt? What explains this?" the second man demanded as he stormed into the small room, forcing Rebekah to walk farther in and closer to the Turk who had entered first.

"The blood is… it is sinful to speak of."

Rebekah sounded modest and embarrassed, acting her part perfectly. Recai liked her more with each moment they spent together. Now, she was in danger and all he could do was grind his teeth and hold his muscles in still readiness. His legs cried out with pain from the uncomfortable position he was in, and his mind screamed at him to do something.

"No, this is not menstrual blood. I am not a stupid man. I suggest you try the truth the next time you speak."

Recai held his breath, his body shaking with the need to act. He bit the pillow in front of him to keep from jumping up and screaming. If he were well he could defend her; Recai had spent his life fencing, boxing, and practicing Karakucak in school leagues. He'd served in the Turkish Army and had even served two years with the elite Egirdir Commando. He was hardly a stranger to a broken nose or twisted ankle, but his injuries were too severe to allow him to be of help.

Rebekah remained silent despite the man's interrogation; her irritation at the morality policemen standing in her home mounted. She simply did not know what to say and, in times like this, found it best to say nothing at all. Let them think her stupid or afraid if they wished. She didn't care so long as they left.

Keeping her head down, she was glad for the eggplant colored burqa her father had bought her. Even her eyes were covered by a strip of lace she could see out of but which did not allow others to see in.

She walked near the second man, hoping to pass by him and either escort them to the door or attempt to get her father's gun. However, instead of stepping out of the way, as courtesy would dictate, the man grabbed her arm roughly. His fingers dug into her flesh, eliciting a gasp.

"You are not telling us everything. We heard there is a man hiding in this town, a man who went missing recently. We need to know where he is, and it seems you know something you are not telling us."

His voice was low and menacing, promising consequences if she refused to help. His grip on her arm tightened and she whimpered. But Rebekah did not raise her head to look at him or answer his questions, she would not be bullied. She would stand tall and resist the evil surrounding her, as her namesake had done so long ago.

"Perhaps you don't know anything, or perhaps you are afraid," the man continued. "The only thing to fear from us is if you lie to us. We are not here to ask about your days and nights spent alone. We are not here to investigate your virginity, only to find this person. He may be in danger. He may be hurt, and we are here to help him, to take him home."

Rebekah shook her head as she continued to look at the floor, a single tear breaking free. The man's threats were not well-veiled, but there was nothing she could do. If she revealed Recai's presence, her punishment may well be worse than any of the things she might endure at the hands of these men. She sent out a thought to her father, hoping he would not blame her for the disgrace she was surely about to suffer.

The man pushed Rebekah back on the cot roughly, which landed her directly on Recai's midsection. Her weight drove a broken rib into his body, puncturing his lung.

As Recai's punctured lung filled with blood, across the desert in Elih, Darya looked out over the city of her birth from the balcony of her penthouse apartment. The glow of the city an ominous backdrop for the minarets atop tall mosque pillars. Cars flew by below her, their light stretching before them, creating an up-lit glow for the buildings surrounding her apartment. This city that had eaten others alive was the catalyst for both her success and her constant frustration.

The sky was orange in the distance as the yellow dust from an impending kum firtinasi, a sandstorm, swept over the desert. Soon she would need to go inside to keep from breathing in too many of the fine particulates. But for now, she watched as destruction rolled toward the city, the distant sound of thunder warning of the danger about to descend.

She ran a hand over her coiffed hair, feeling the flatness her headscarf had left behind. She hated having to cover in public, but her uncle's "morality police" made it necessary. Mayor Mahmet Yilmaz was her father's younger brother and a constant presence in her life. And even though she was afforded many freedoms by her familial ties as the niece of the mayor of Elih, she could not be seen to publicly flaunt her status. And so her styled hair and expensive clothes were hidden away, displayed only behind closed doors.

Darya was stuck in a limbo of sorts; her ambitions for prestige and power were undermined by her gender. She saw no justification for the restrictions on her. Indeed, they were necessary for the lower class and for the people out in the deserts. These rules helped keep peace—or so her uncle claimed. If true, then so be it; she had no interest in the plights of others anyway. But the fabric of her hijab chafed at her ego and pride.

Tightening her hands around the railing of the balcony she leaned out, inhaling the last bits of fresh air there would be for days. When the storm hit, the sky would be blotted out for hours, the sun covered by sand, blanketing the city into darkness. After the winds died down the rain would begin, but not the purifying rain the city so desperately needed. The water would only serve to solidify the grime where it lay. The people in the city would be wiping every surface to remove sand and grit until, inevitably, the next storm would wash over.

Tasting the electricity in the air, she cursed inwardly at the weather for keeping her inside. Her external conditions mirrored her life: forced to live behind closed doors, existing in secret, moving her chess pieces from the shadows so in the end, she got what she wanted. She was no one in the world outside, no one would know her on sight and her name held no awe. Here, behind the veil of a computer screen and a pseudonym, she was powerful and commanded respect.

Turning back toward her apartment, she approached the French doors that served as gates to her prison of luxury. Just as Darya stepped inside to change for the night's charity event, lightning slashed through the distant sandstorm.

While Darya prepared for the inevitable sandstorm, Recai involuntarily lurched up, forcing the broken rib farther into his chest. His attempts to` breathe came out as a crackling, gasping sound as his pierced lung began to deflate.

"Recai!"

Rebekah reached for him.

"You whore of a liar!"

One of the RTK men grabbed Rebekah's arm. She lashed out, whipping around and slapping him solidly in the face.

"Don't hurt her…!" Recai wheezed from the bed, his body fighting desperately for oxygen.

He forced himself to sit up but the pain in his chest was unbearable. The second man stepped forward and pulled the sheet off of Recai's body.

"In only bed clothes!" the second man exclaimed as he turned his back on Recai. "Alone with a man in this state of undress. What kind of woman are you?"

Rebekah struggled against the RTK officer's tight grip, but she was unable to break away. Instead, she simply spit at the insult. Recai reached forward, enduring a pain so complete he felt certain he would pass out. Slowly his hand rose toward the pistol holstered in the officer's belt. Inches from the weapon, Recai leaned farther forward, forcing his body to succumb to the demands of his soul.

"Mahmoud!" the man holding Rebekah called, bringing his companion's attention to Recai. Mahmoud turned around quickly and backhanded Recai. He flew back against the wall, hitting his head against the hard plaster. The wound on his cheek opened and waves of nausea swept over him. Moaning, Recai briefly shut his eyes, wishing he was anywhere else. Doing anything else. His consciousness threatened to fall under the surface of pain but Rebekah's voice calling out brought him back.

"You killed him!" Rebekah screamed, fearing the worst. "Recai! Don't you know he's already hurt?"

Her cries were met with a cruelty that neither Rebekah nor Recai could have anticipated. The first officer, called Mahmoud, backhanded her, snapping her head back.

"You cry for your lover?" he sneered. "Where is your father? Where is your mother? Is there no one here to protect you from your female lusts?"

"No…" Recai moaned.

"Answer me, you whore!"

Rebekah received another blow but did not call out; she did not answer her abuser or submit to his inquisition. Recai inched himself forward as Mahmoud threw Rebekah to the floor. Her elbow hit the concrete with a cracking noise. Still covered by her burqa, it was impossible for Recai to see if she was in pain or if tears had escaped from her deep brown eyes. The lace over her face hid her, but he felt her gaze upon him.

"The Holy Prophet said 'Whenever a man is alone with a woman, the Devil makes a third'," Mahmoud spat the verse, glaring down at the dark purple pile of cloth that hid Rebekah from view.

"There has been no sin!" Recai rasped, attempting to stand by sheer force of will. His knee screamed in protest as he pulled himself up. Reaching his feet he stood in defiance, only to be pistol-whipped back to the cot by the second RTK officer who stood nearest him.

"And yet you lie here in a state of undress alone with a Jew woman?"

"Why were you looking for me?" Recai asked, hoping to pull their attention away from Rebekah. Perhaps they would finish what they started and kill him and leave her alone. His voice was weak as he fought for breath.

"We are looking for those who offend the Prophet; here we have found two."

Mahmoud reached down and roughly pulled Rebekah to her feet. She stood limply at his side, a marionette of fabric and bones.

"No, you said you were looking for a man who was missing, who may be hurt. How did you know about me? How did you know I was in the desert?"

"Perhaps you are not the man we were looking for."

Mahmoud's grip on Rebekah's arm tightened, causing a small whimper.

"Perhaps you are simply a weak man who succumbed to the temptations of the flesh that this whore presented to you? Perhaps you are innocent of any wrongdoing, a victim, and need only repent."

"Is this what happened?" the first RTK officer inquired, peering at Recai through slanted eyes. "Were you tempted by this woman? We are looking only to punish those who merit it. If you were tempted and surrendered to the weakness of the flesh, all you must do is repent. Allah is merciful in his wisdom."

"No. There is no sin here," Recai insisted.

"And you, can you explain this man, dressed in his bed clothes?" He asked, turning his attention on Rebekah.

"He was injured." Her voice a tenuous whisper, "I cared for him in his need. He would have died without our help."

"And so you tended to his needs? Caring for his body?" Mahmoud pressed.

"I...no...I sought only to help ease his pain."

"This is a house of sin!" the other, nameless, RTK officer roared. Recai noticed for the first time that there was a tattoo on his neck—eyes of ink peered out at him over the collar of the man's shirt.

"No...!" Recai tried to explain.

"Do you say the girl is lying?" the officer pressed.

The tattooed officer's attention turned to Recai again, and he leaned down closer, his breath hot and moist against Recai's face.

"She tells the truth...you twist the meaning," Recai replied.

"Well, we shall have to ensure we are hearing the truth." Cruelty glinted in the officer's eyes as he smiled. "And you shall watch."

"No!"

Recai lurched forward, willing his body to fight, to defend Rebekah. Using all of his energy he delivered one weak blow to the tattooed man's chest. His body was beaten and broken and lacking in oxygen; he simply could not fight.

Laughing mirthlessly, the man punched Recai solidly in the jaw, cracking the joint. Tears sprang to Recai's eyes. Falling backwards he slumped against the wall. The metallic taste of blood filled his mouth. His lip had been split when it slammed against his teeth from the officer's violent blow. Blood fell from the wound Rebekah had stitched up, dripping down the side of his face, staining his skin.

"We are the servants of Allah," the inked officer taunted as he stood up and delivered a kick directly to Recai's middle, eliciting a cry. The impact pulled Recai in on himself. He huddled tightly on the bed, unable to retaliate. The pain from his ribs tore through him, shattering his focus. All he could make out were snake eyes that were part of his attacker's tattoo.

The officer continued, "We follow the example of Ali who, upon requiring a slave girl to tell the truth, beat her before allowing her to testify to The Prophet."

"No...." Recai wheezed as he watched the man's hand rise in the air before delivering the first of many blows to Rebekah's form.

"In delivering punishment, The Prophet tells us 'Let not compassion move you in their case'."

He took a measured step toward Rebekah, ominous purpose glinting in his eyes. Mahmoud gripped her upper arms firmly, holding her still.

The tattooed officer beat her despite Recai's screams, despite his admission that the indiscretion was his fault, and despite his desperate plea for them to punish him and show her mercy. He beat her until her body slumped forward, no longer possessing the strength to hold her own weight. He beat her until her cries of pain waned and only a glimmer of consciousness remained.

"The devil take you!" Recai spat at the officers.

Mahmoud threw Rebekah's body on the cot where Recai was slowly suffocating. He tried to pull her to him, but she shook her head.

"No, give them no justification for their sin," she whispered, wanting there to be no appearance of intimacy between them.

"The whore speaks," Mahmoud said with a smile.

"I believe she is trying to tempt you, brother." The tattooed officer who had delivered Rebekah's beating clapped Mahmoud on the shoulder.

"I believe she has not yet learned her place," Mahmoud agreed with a cock of his head and a lusty curl of his lips. "She will need to be shown."

Mahmoud reached down and pulled Rebekah's lower body off of the bed so that she lay on her stomach, her knees upon the hard floor.

The wind outside picked up and thunder rumbled in the distance. The distinctive sound of sand beating against the house began slowly at first, but grew steadily until the onslaught was deafening. Electricity crackled in the air.

Mahmoud lifted the eggplant colored burqa Hasad had bought for his only living child, revealing her modest blue house dress. Rebekah stifled a cry as Recai screamed into the air. The other officer held a knife to Recai's neck, holding him in place, forcing him to watch as Mahmoud exposed her tender virgin skin.

Mahmoud loomed behind Rebekah as he unzipped his pants. Sand slammed into the house, the force shaking the jars on the shelves as the electricity flickered in and out, creating a strobe effect on the brutal scene. Recai's mind revolted against the sight. He wanted to shut it out, pass out, disappear into the oblivion of unconsciousness. Terror shone from Rebekah's eyes behind the lace mask. Recai was so close to her that he could see through the veil to her deep brown eyes.

Her fear ripped at Recai when her eyes opened wide at Mahmoud brutally entered her. Rebekah buried her face into the cot but her muffled scream pierced the air. The rapist moved quickly, panting as he pounded into her, her fear intoxicating him.

"Stop!" Recai begged, earning the laughter of the tattooed officer who held the knife to his throat.

"Watch, see what happens to those who defy the RTK," he hissed.

"How can you claim to do the work of Allah?" he begged.

Recai's tears fell freely as he watched their brutality. Pain saturated the air as Mahmoud continued his assault on Rebekah's body.

"How can you lie here, undressed in the home of a Jew?" the officer screamed, tightening the knife against Recai's neck, piercing his skin.

"Kill me! Just let her go!"

Recai sobbed for Rebekah and Hasad, and for all of the others who were so mistreated by the cruelty and corruption of his city. He thought he had known how brutal life could be. His own insulated world had allowed him distance from this reality, sanitizing and mocking the sins of the RTK. Now he saw the true nature of evil before him.

Leaning into the knife, Recai prayed for his own death until he saw Rebekah's eyes lock onto his from behind the strip of lace. She was so close and yet he could not reach her. Her voice broke from the pain as the monster continued to rip through her body. Recai was only a witness to this offense against Allah. Holding her eyes, he did the only thing he could to try and keep her sane in this insane moment.

His tears fell but he never looked away, never shielded himself from her agony, knowing that they would forever be bound together because of this moment. When her pain became more than she could bear alone, she grasped his leg, digging her nails into his flesh until she drew blood. He bled for her willingly.

He whispered to her his apology and regret. She was the second woman in his useless life that he was unable to save. He had watched his mother throw herself into the sea and he couldn't stop her; and now Rebekah was suffering the worst humiliation possible and he couldn't even sit up.

He vowed to her and to himself that she would be safe with him. That no matter what was done to her now, he would always protect and honor her. He swore to marry her when this was over, so she would never be alone or afraid. In his eyes she bore no shame for the injustice being done to her body. He cried when she screamed, and reached for her when she began to fade from consciousness due to the assault on her body.

Again and again Rebekah was violated by the men who had invaded her home; they used her until her body was bloody and broken. Recai never looked away, forcing himself to bear witness to her pain, promising to repay their cruelty tenfold.

When the two RTK agents were done with her they asked Rebekah again: "Do you repent? Do you admit your sinful ways?"

But she lay silent.

"You demons," Recai spat, his final in a series of curses.

His outburst was rewarded with another blow to his head. The sandstorm outside had passed over them, leaving only the distant thunder and charged air. Soon the rain would fall; Recai prayed it would wash away the pain of the night.

"Jew-Bitch! You pay for your sin." Mahmoud growled menacingly.

"I have committed no sin, but I have had sin committed upon me," Rebekah whispered hoarsely.

And like a flash of lightning, the knife that had been held to Recai's neck reached out and sliced through the purple fabric around her neck. Warmth spread over Recai's legs as her life spilled from her wound.

His voice eclipsed all thought as he sobbed, reaching for her, attempting to pull her to him. But his body refused to comply, and instead of holding her in her last moments he watched as the light left her eyes. Her gaze was glassy and distant as she passed on from this world. Her blood seeped out, darkening her burqa to black.

"What have you done?" Mahmoud demanded as he pulled the tattooed man away from Rebekah's body. The two RTK officers whispered furtively while Recai keened in mourning. When his screams rose in intensity, they struck him one last time upon the head, forcing him to finally submit to the darkness.

Prominent Business Man Missing

Recai Osman, the only son of the late Pinar Osman and missing Baris Osman, was last seen leaving the illustrious Bozoogullari Hotel two weeks ago. Reported missing by the Board of Directors, the young heir to the multi-billion-

Euro corporation Osman Enterprises, is presumed dead. Anyone with any information on his whereabouts is encouraged to report directly to the RTK.

At this time, Osman Enterprises has made no official statement to the press, but is assuring stockholders that the company will continue to operate consistent with the high Osman standards the entire community has come to rely upon.

Leaving behind no living relatives, the legacy of the Osman family ends in ashes.

PART 2

"ON YOUR BELLY YOU SHALL CRAWL, AND DUST YOU SHALL EAT,
ALL THE DAYS OF YOUR LIFE"

Genesis 3:14

THREE YEARS LATER

Darya stepped away from the mirror behind the row of sinks after applying her lipstick one final time. Her hijab lay discarded and forgotten on the tiled floor. The flatness of her hair was finally fixed and her locks flowed freely down her back, their dark, nearly black hue shining against her white clothes. Spinning, she took one last look to admire herself in the floor-length mirror. She wore red high heels with high-waisted, snug white pants that emphasized her long legs. The matching white halter contrasted sharply with her honey-brown skin. She was ready.

It had been so long since she'd been able to attend a public event. Darya expected to make her entrance memorable. Tonight was the first time she'd been out since she'd assumed control of the finances of her uncle's business venture, and although that wasn't publicly known, the resulting pride swelled within her. At twenty-three years old, this was the first time she'd be seen as a woman and not a child.

She left the ladies' room smelling like spicy flowers and the night-cooled desert. Darya was beautiful. Her vanity screamed for her to be seen but she had been born into the wrong world at the wrong time. *Tonight though.* Tonight she was going to shine.

The main entrance to the Bozoogullari Hotel's ballroom was unimpressive. Two large double doors with no windows or decoration stood at the end of a dark hall off the grand but plain foyer. The doors remained closed, opening only as attendees for the events were admitted entrance. The lobby had been designed

45

using sparse decorations and white marble, which shone from within even in the evening light. Darya's steps echoed against the cavernous hallways. Nothing about the hotel welcomed loitering or conversation.

Tonight, the elite of Elih were celebrating her uncle's fifteenth year as mayor, and behind those heavy doors the restrictions he imposed on the city were temporarily lifted. There would be drinking and dancing. There would be fashionable women showing off their beauty. Darya couldn't wait to be one of them.

An RTK guard stationed in front of the entrance took the names of all who entered. No one rose above his scrutiny; if you were not on the list, admittance would be denied. She approached the guard with the arrogance of one who had her every demand catered to. He gazed warily over his dark glasses. RTK officers were all the same, so easily manipulated by the hint of seduction.

"Assalamu Alaikum, Sister," he greeted, his eyes focused on the low dip of her neckline.

"Walaikum as salaam, Brother. I am here for the celebration."

The guard raised an eyebrow and lifted his attention to her face. He stood up from his stool and pulled the attendee list out of the side pocket of his military-issue cargo pants.

"You were invited?"

Darya laughed. "Of course." Her back straightened as she spoke.

"You are here without an escort."

The guard folded the list and slipped it back into his pocket. Darya stared at him. Silence echoed in the great hall as she waited, daring him with sharp eyes to speak his mind.

"Sister, without an escort, it would be improper for you to attend such an event."

"The only impropriety here is your refusal to allow me inside."

"Do you question me?"

His eyes were hard as he took off his glasses and stared at her. The authority of men was rarely questioned, let alone that of an RTK officer. Darya was a tall woman, but the guard stood well over 180 centimeters and too close for her not to notice the stench of whiskey on his breath. This defender of her uncle's strict interpretation of Shariah law seemed to feel no need to abide by the sacred rules himself as he clearly had indulged in the forbidden drink.

"No, I will inform my uncle of your…"

Darya reached for the door but the guard's hand, hard on her wrist, stopped her cold.

"Your hand, sir."

She spoke softly, as was expected, but lifted her eyes to meet his without flinching.

"Your eyes, Sister…" He brought himself closer to her, the heat of his breath warm against her skin. "Your eyes are striking. So dark there is almost no pupil. Perhaps I should consider escorting you myself?"

The guard's other hand came to rest on her hip. Darya tensed, but she refused to look away. His touch was an offense to her and her family, but to object now would only worsen the situation. The man's threat lay coiled beneath the surface of his words, needing only the slightest provocation to burst forth in violent attack.

"I need no escort," she stated calmly, as the man's hand roamed down her hip.

"You are here uncovered, showing the world what you have to offer. Without an escort, that could be very dangerous."

"Did you not hear me? I need no escort."

She stepped away from him forcefully, breaking his hold on her.

The guard took one step forward. His fist clenched as he wrestled with his desire and his duty. He appraised her lustfully

47

then grunted. Stepping back to his post, the guard's mouth twisted into a cruel smile.

"Then I'm afraid I will not be able to admit you inside."

"Wh...what?"

Darya stumbled over the word, having expected the liberal atmosphere of the party to extend to its admittance. His simple refusal stunned her. When she was hidden behind fabric or heavy doors, her gender didn't stand in her way. But standing before him, exposed, her weakness was the only thing he saw. Behind the veil of anonymity she escaped confinement. Faced with its reality, the sharp corners of her prison scratched at her psyche.

The guard sat back down on his stool and focused his attention on the foyer behind her, her presence no longer of concern. The music from behind the heavy doors drifted into the hall, adding an insulting punctuation to her humiliation.

Anger swarmed in her mind, threatening to break loose. Frustrated and embarrassed, she wanted to lash out, punch him, rip at his face with her freshly painted nails until he bled across the white marble floor. She wanted to demand he see who she was—that she was important. Were she a man she would teach him what it meant to be in control. Instead, she straightened her top and smoothed her hair.

"I will be right back, Brother."

Her voice was thick with anger and malice. As she glared at him, the guard stood up without taking notice of her to greet someone approaching.

"Assalamu Alaikum, may I have your name?" he said formally.

Darya turned to see a striking man standing a few paces behind her, dressed in a tailored suit that appeared custom made. His closely trimmed, auburn-red beard allowed his dark skin to shine beneath the unique hue. A scar ran along his right cheek, lighter than the rest of his flesh, as though an eraser had been taken to his brown skin. But his eyes arrested her attention. They were green and vibrant, and when they drifted to hers they did not stray to molest her body with their gaze. Instead, he smiled and bowed his head in respectful greeting, ignoring the officer until it suited him to respond.

"Recai," the man stated keeping his eyes on Darya. He lifted his back straighter before squaring his shoulders and facing the guard. "Recai Osman."

"Osman?" the guard inquired, checking the names on the list. "I'm sorry sir; there is no Osman on the list."

"No?" Recai asked calmly, holding the guard's gaze steadily until the man looked away. Recai had the expectation and breeding of someone not often denied.

"I..." the guard stammered, uncomfortable under the piercing eyes of the strange man before him. "I'm sorry sir. There is no Osman."

"You will need to check again, or perhaps contact your superior."

Recai smiled, his tone neither kind nor inviting, giving his face a subtle cruelty Darya found exciting.

Osman... Darya's mind whirled in an attempt to place the name. Only one family with that name wielded the kind of power needed to enter this party uninvited, and that entire family was lost. The mother shamed, died years ago, the father had disappeared soon after. And the son disappeared, leaving no trace.

Her gaze snapped back to Recai.

"No, there's nothing on the list, I cannot—" the guard said, before Darya interrupted him.

"Recai?"

Darya sidled up to the handsome man with the impossibly familiar name.

"Would you care to be my escort this evening? Apparently, I am required to have one."

49

Darya glared at the guard before intimately wrapping her hand around Recai's upper arm.

"I would be honored." Recai lowered his head again, accepting her invitation.

His voice was low and his accent strange. *Kurdish, Turkish, American, English, perhaps even a hint of French. Or perhaps from one of the African colonies?* So many inflections intermingling made his tone impossible for Darya to place.

"Sister," the guard began, looking at Darya's cleavage again, his intentions clear: if she was to be compromised tonight he expected to be the one doing the compromising. But this time, she had her required escort and was not about to deal with the guard's insults.

"What is your name?" she demanded.

"I...."

"Name!"

Darya released Recai's arm and stepped in front of him. There was nothing—nothing—he could say now to refuse her entry. She would have him hung by his thumbs for touching her, or perhaps have his hand cut off, or find out if he had a sister. Or daughter.

The guard pulled his lip back in an insolent sneer at her tone.

"Fahri Kaya."

"Well Brother Kaya, I will be sure to let Captain Sener know how you performed your duties tonight. It is important we all keep vigil against the crowding evils of the outside world. Every incident of indecency must be reported, don't you think?" Darya said, her voice soft and calm as she stretched out her threat, pulling it taut around his neck.

"You are clearly not a woman to be trifled with," Recai chuckled below his breath as she placed her arm back in his before they entered the large ballroom arm in arm.

Darya's ego cheered at the recognition and compliment in his words. She yearned for a life in which all men looked at her as a force of nature not to be trifled with, to be able to stand outside in the wind, her hair uncovered, and scream to the sky that she had arrived. Tonight she would step out of her confinement and into the world of prestige and power she longed to join. No longer a girl, but a king-whisperer and a power unto herself.

Once inside, Darya took a deep breath. The hall was beautiful, nothing like the dreary foyer behind them. The man on her arm was handsome and mysterious, adding to the image of power she hoped to portray. Arched columns supporting a balcony surrounded the large room. Banners in every imaginable color hung in celebration of each year of her uncle's achievements, filling the space with a sense of festivity. She had been here years ago for one of her cousin's weddings, to his second wife, but her memory did not do it justice.

White marble shone from floor to ceiling. Teardrop chandeliers hung low over the guests, casting a soft glow over the room. The ornate beauty of the decor highlighted the vivid colors of the guests' attire. *No drab black or navy burqas tonight!* Before her stood everyone who had profited under the rule of Mayor Yilmaz. She soon lost herself in the beauty of possibilities.

Darya took in the warm light shining down from five large chandeliers above. Familiar music swelled above the hum of voices filling the room. Before her was a scene out of a fairy tale, where princes were real and princesses had the freedom to run in the garden. With a sigh, she looked up at the pleasant surprise the night had brought her.

Tonight, the elite of the city were celebrating the absolute power Mayor Yilmaz wielded over his city. Mayor Yilmaz, whose only contributions to the place he now ruled were fear and ignorance. Those in attendance of this party were the beneficiaries of his rule, the highest class, living off the oppression of the people beneath them on the food chain. Men drank martinis while women spoke animatedly. The dark night that covered the city was forgotten.

Beside Darya, Recai's face tightened as his narrowed eyes roamed the crowd.

Osman Enterprises had been the backbone of Elih. Recai's family had overseen the creation of foundations and interest-free banks for those who had never qualified in the past. Baris Osman never doubted his ability to change the system and help the people he loved achieve more. Recai had been young when his father disappeared, but he never doubted that Baris was a hero. The shadow of the father lost still haunted Recai, heading off any ambition of his own.

At one time, money had flowed in from the Turkish government. And what the government didn't provide, Osman Enterprises did. Recai's mother was a vision of humility and inner strength, the perfect combination of Muslim modesty and Kurdish wisdom. Their marriage was controversial. A Turk and a Kurd—it was unthinkable, especially in the circles in which they ran. But love somehow finds a way. Recai's birth symbolized unity to the people and his existence came to mean more than any of his accomplishments.

Ethnic divisions were ignored and the feuds of generations past forgotten. Prosperity has a way of bringing even the more ardent enemies together. Schools were built in the border towns, and water was clean and plentiful. Anything was possible with only the willingness to work hard and a dream under your belt.

Osman Enterprises' wealth and generosity gave entrepreneurs the opportunity to explore their dreams while it provided help to those in need. Turkey had allowed Elih to run itself, diverting government funds to other cities that did not have such generous benefactors, forgetting about the insular eastern city. The Osmans gave generously, saying Allah had given them the mission of caring for his people, and their reward in Heaven and on Earth would outshine any loss their company incurred. The company pulled profits every year, despite the outpouring of funds.

The night tragedy and shame fell upon the Osman family, Recai had been frightened. His parents never fought and his mother certainly never raised her voice. He had laid in bed, listening as their angry words filtered though the cabin, muted so that he could not make out their meaning. Once they stopped and he heard his father slam the door to his quarters, Recai crawled out of bed to investigate. On deck he found his mother, dressed in blue, standing on the helm of the boat. He watched as she held out her arms, embracing the ancient Kurdish god. Her people knew loss, they knew oblivion and abandonment, but Recai had never seen his mother look so empty.

There was no discernible shift in her body or change in the direction of the wind. There was nothing to indicate that suddenly everything would change. Recai screamed as his mother stepped off the edge into the open sea, its ebony abyss swallowing her before he even reached the railing.

Baris disappeared under suspicion of foul play. Recai watched the media declare his father a murderer and a coward. He knew his mother had jumped, but he was too young to speak out and defend his father's reputation. And, in truth, some part of him wondered if perhaps his father wasn't to blame. Alone with his questions and fears his heart turned away from the warmth of his community.

The suspicion was enough to give Yilmaz the ammunition he needed to declare that Elih needed a ruler who would follow Shariah law. He campaigned against the absent Baris because the only one he really needed to defeat was the icon of a savior.

Recai watched as Yilmaz abused and inflated the teachings of Islam, but he was unable to protest. Over the years his own faith faded, unable to keep its spark under the assault of lies from the RTK. He had money but no power. He had knowledge but no wisdom. Recai's grief over the loss of his mother had dulled over the years. While he never understood her reasons, he believed his mother loved him despite taking her own life. But he'd never moved past the loss of his father.

Recai inherited the business after his father left. In the face of all of the controversy surrounding Pinar's death, the money stopped flowing. Corporate leaders ran their businesses tightly, ceasing the abundant loans and demanding repayment on strict terms. People who had been promised help with their businesses were abandoned to their own means, and Recai grew up surrounded by his parents' wealth as family after family fell into poverty.

Schools decayed and sat deserted as the lofty aspirations of social services were forgotten. The city had no choice but to close everything down. Embittered and angry, the people of the city needed a new hero. Recai was barely a teenager when the community turned to the stricter interpretations of their religion. They rigidly held on to the only thing they believed could save them from the spreading decimation of the city. Fear and desperation drove the city straight into the ambitious arms of Mahmet Yilmaz.

And now Mayor Mahmet Yilmaz's sixteenth unopposed term as mayor was beginning. When elected into power, the city had fallen from its prime. The loose morals and divided priorities of a people lost opened the door for corruption. Crumbling under its own weight, the city needed a savior, and Yilmaz had made sure to be the one to stand as Atlas.

In the streets of Elih, no one dared speak a word against him. His draconian tactics stifled the people's voices and minds. The slow spread of oppression had gone unnoticed until it was too late. And now Recai found himself standing in a room among the worst offenders.

Darya squeezed Recai's arm gently, bringing him back from his meandering thoughts.

"A bit overwhelming isn't it?" she breathed.

"I haven't spent much time around crowds recently. I've been…traveling."

Recai's voice had a scratched timbre, as if it had gone too long unused.

"Well, I never get to be in crowds," she offered, smiling. "So we must keep each other safe."

"I find it difficult to believe a mere crowd would intimidate the likes of you."

"Intimidate, no. But the unfamiliar is always worthy of skepticism."

Darya demurely raised her chin as she looked up at him.

"Yes," Recai smiled in return, unable to resist her infectious enthusiasm. "I guess we will brave the unknown together. It appears I am your escort after all."

With another squeeze of his arm, Darya led the mysterious man away from the main door and into the crowd. They entered the celebration arm in arm. Numerous eyes focused on them, forcing Darya to swallow a lump of anticipation in her throat. Whispers trailed behind them, but she had to strain her ears to make out the words.

"Gossiping old berbat kimse." Darya's eyes sparkled with delight. That she was here at all was news, and her handsome escort—who may or may not be the ghost of a son returned—only added to the mystery.

"Is there intrigue afoot?" Recai teased.

"There is always intrigue afoot, is there not? This is the den of traitors, and all here are out for their thirty pieces of silver," Darya whispered.

Recai laughed—a loud, unrestrained sound that for a moment drowned out his pain.

"Yes. Yes, I guess that's so."

The air was lighter with his laughter suspended around them, blocking the curious looks. As they bantered, a waiter walked past with sparkling flutes of champagne.

"Champagne...."

Darya watched the waiter longingly, having never tasted the infamous drink. Recai called impulsively after the man, who turned, head bowed, and offered them a glass.

"Darya, may I offer you a glass of champagne?" Recai gestured with a flourish of his hand.

Flirting came easily to her, a means to an end. She had always approached men with a focused determination, interested only in what would be gained or accomplished with each entanglement. But this strange man made an unfamiliar feeling bubble up inside of her she wasn't entirely sure she liked. Recai took two glasses before dismissing the waiter.

"A drink will help soothe the frayed nerves of an anxious guest," he said, handing her one of the glasses.

As she took the flute, her fingers brushed against his. Only the lightest of touches, but it reached deep into her. Darya's smile quirked to the side and a tingle ran down her spine, catching her off guard. Cautiously she sipped the carbonated wine, and the bubbles tickled her tongue as she swallowed.

"I've never had anything like this before," she admitted.

"No?"

"I'm afraid you might think me quite sheltered."

"We should all be so lucky."

Recai's voice was dark, as if a storm brewed just beneath the surface of his words. Darya did not shrink away from the ugly things in this world, but she did not like the color of his eyes as he spoke.

"I'm sorry," Recai closed his eyes before looking at her again. When he did, it was with a cloaking calm. "Are you hungry? Or perhaps there is someone you are meeting here?"

"No, no one," she admitted. "I would like to speak with plenty of them, but the music is loud and the night is full of unexpected surprises."

"Indeed it is."

"I'd much prefer to know more about you, Bey Osman. But first, please excuse me a moment. I need to make a brief phone call."

"Of course, I'm sorry for monopolizing you."

"I'll only be a moment."

Darya turned away and rushed to the outskirts of the crowd eager to make the call that would teach the guard Fahri Kaya the error he had made in threatening her. Her power may exist behind a veil, but its ramifications could be felt in the heart of her enemies. Pulling a small cell phone from her purse she quickly dialed the number she knew so well. On the other end of the line a gruff voice answered. It was the voice of the only person who knew who she really was.

When her call was complete and she was satisfied, she returned to the side of Recai Osman.

Darya wrapped her hand around his arm, allowing her fingers to grip him tightly as she came to stand closer. Recai was unlike anyone she had met before. She sensed a strength and violence warring beneath his façade. *What would he be if he let go?* She leaned against his strong frame and a tingle of anticipation spread out from her spine.

Standing here with Darya, his thoughts meandered back to his years in the desert. His years alone after he lost he lost Rebekah, after he lost everything. Recai felt confident in his decision to return home: revenge, justification. The desert had stilled his heart but the press of bodies and sounds within the ballroom made him feel nervous and unprepared. He never attended these functions when his position within the Osman Empire called for; he was always too young or too disinterested.

He had been near death when Kurdish nomads found him, burned and alone. Someone had dragged his body deep into the desert and left him with nothing but a canteen. He'd awoken to their voices, calling him back from oblivion. They spoke his mother's language and offered him understanding without ever asking why he was lying in the sand wearing nothing but blood-soaked sleeping pants.

For three years he wore black, wandered with Kurdish nomads, and let his beard grow. Hundreds of miles of sand passed beneath his feet and months of silence filled his ears, but despite his reflection, peace remained always out of reach.

He found moments of calm, the closest thing he could find to serenity, inevitably broken by the sudden smell of

Rebekah's skin on the desert breeze or the subtle taste of her tears in the rain. Somewhere between life and death his heart had made a home for them. A love tied him to her so strongly he feared it would overwhelm him and drag him beneath the surface into a dark abyss.

Over the years, Recai found he could no longer sleep through the night. His dreams danced within his mind, leaving him restless and frustrated. Every night he would lay awake for hours, finally submitting to sleep only to wake just before her veil would lift. He couldn't cry; he had no tears left. He couldn't fight; his body had been broken. He couldn't sleep; he had no peace. The hole in his chest was ragged and raw and never did close, although the scars on his flesh eventually faded.

One night, as the others drifted to their beds he walked alone into the heart of the desert one more time, leaving behind no trace, sand filling in his footprints. The city called to him, her lights dim in the distance. He traveled by night, and during the harsh light of day he would sleep for the few hours that he could. He continued for days until he reached the civilization he had abandoned. His dreams remained vivid and he often woke with a scream on his lips, images of fire and the dead stare of beautiful brown eyes in his mind.

Recai enjoyed Darya's attention, but more than that he was elated his plan was proving easier to execute than expected. The guard had his name. He relied on that being enough for word to spread that the son of Baris Osman had returned from the dead. Darya also drew attention to them; she was clearly someone of importance, or at least curiosity. How better to re-enter the world than to be seen with this striking woman, who stood almost as tall as himself? Now he had only to allow word of his presence to spread slowly through the crowd. Dead men make the most intriguing party guests.

His plan to attend tonight's event was sound. He would watch the reactions of those around him and see who spoke of his past and who ignored his return. A part of him hoped the men who had abandoned him in the desert, who had destroyed so much, would recognize him and attempt to finish what they began. This time, he would not be so easily subdued.

"You have been away from home for a long time?" Darya inquired, tilting her head up to face him, her smile bright and her lips red.

"What?" Recai's reply was too sharp.

He had lost some of the grooming of his youth during his time in the desert. But the memory of his mother kept his back straight and his shoulders broad. He would do her legacy right.

"You said you hadn't been in crowds much recently."

"Oh, yes."

He took a sip of his champagne, refocusing and pulling his attention back into the present.

"You couldn't have been in Elih, if there were no crowds!"

Darya was beautiful, no doubt about that. Her face was sharp: pointed chin, dramatic coloring, and rolling layers of thick hair. Put together, each feature enhanced and softened the others, giving her a look of ancient beauty. She was elegant and poised with a fierce gaze.

"No, no, I've been on a bit of a hajj I guess you would say." Recai chuckled, in spite of himself.

"You've been to Mecca?" Darya asked excitedly. Her feet itched to explore the world, to see the sky from anywhere but her penthouse balcony.

"Ahh, no, not a real Hajj. More of a personal quest."

"You've been lost."

She stated it as a fact.

"And you are very insightful."

He turned to face her as he spoke, allowing her attention to occupy him. Without thinking, Recai reached out and placed his hand gently on the waist of the woman before him. With her hand still on his arm they stood close, close enough that Recai could smell her spicy perfume and the undertones of sandalwood oil. Music surrounded them, sealing the illusion that they were alone in the crowd.

The two lost themselves. They stood outside of their customs and culture, souls yearning for more, beyond the constraints their worlds placed on them. Both had all of the privilege and power to have almost anything they wanted, but each was chained to a rock which slowly pulled them under the surface.

The sitar blended with an electronic beat while a woman sang in Bulgarian, weaving a traditional sound with modern style. People had begun dancing in the center of the room; the wait staff served golden glasses of champagne and other liquors as fast as they could be poured.

Recai placed his other hand on Darya's hip and stepped closer to her.

He split in two, feeling as though sinew and muscle were ripping away from his heart. His body could not let go of the past, even for a moment. With a sigh he dropped his hands and stepped away from her embrace, his skin cold.

"Something has hurt you," Darya surmised with her usual confidence. "I'm sorry."

"No…" Recai felt the flush of shame rush to his cheeks. "Please, I… Don't be sorry."

He spoke earnestly in a world where honesty was rare, and it filled her with joy.

"There is nothing so awful that time and faith can't overcome. That's what they tell us, isn't it? Well Recai, between you and me, they lied. Some things cannot be overcome. It's how we continue on in spite of them that matters."

They danced in and out of each other's reach through the night. Recai would take a step forward, only to retreat when Darya found the courage to meet his advance. Outside, the stars were on fire as they moved slowly across the sky. To them, the city was a million miles away from the horrors of his past. It was seductive to forget, to rewrite history, for Recai to change his past with the more benign story of having been on a spiritual quest instead of a desperate attempt to escape life.

Eventually, Darya left him to join a group of women. While with Recai her whispered words spoke of judgment and annoyance, but publicly she smiled and laughed easily. He watched as she would answer a question with a smile, her head nodding toward him. No one spoke to him; had he changed so much during his years away? Could no one recognize him anymore? Sand had hardened his hands and the sun had leathered his skin, but the green of his eyes and hue of his beard were enough for anyone to know it was him. Darya weaved her way through the crowd until she disappeared out of his line of sight.

Recai approached the bar and ordered a bourbon from an aging bartender. He watched as the guards shifted closer to his position and the guests eyed him with speculation. In the end, everyone left him alone. No one knew what to say to a ghost.

Drink in hand, Recai leaned against the bar, allowing the dulcet tones of the acoustic guitar to calm his nerves. He rubbed his eyes before taking a sip, allowing the spicy liquor to burn his mouth and throat.

"Effendi, sit here." A young woman working as a waitress for the evening called respectfully to the old bartender, when he stepped into the back room. The term of endearment was not lost on him and he smiled in response. He rubbed his hands and reminded her so much of her aging mother that she couldn't help but make the spontaneous offer.

The waitress wore a long black skirt and a tightly fitted white blouse. Her chestnut hair was pulled back into a tight ponytail and hung loose down her back. Hijabs were not allowed at the mayor's celebration. Despite initially looking forward to being without it, she found herself feeling exposed and cold. Her ears were uncomfortable from the touch of the breeze.

"Maryam, you are kind to an old man," he said as he lowered himself heavily onto the backless stool.

"Eh, the unkindness of the world far outweighs one offered seat."

"Yes it does my dear, yes it does."

The old man flexed his aching fingers, stretching the scar tissue across his bones.

"Besides," Maryam stretched and yawned without covering her mouth. "I'll never get up if left to my own desires. I could sit and let the night's work fade away, leaving the 'yes ma'ams' and 'of course sirs' to the others."

She mimicked the voices of the other waitresses as she spoke, making the old man reveal the first honest smile he may have made in years.

"Just keep your hands where the women can see them and your other assets where the men cannot, and the night will be over before you know it," he remarked.

"Effendi, why are you working here?" Maryam asked, ignoring rules of courtesy and custom to assuage her curiosity. "Don't you have children to work while you sit at home in the evenings?"

Maryam thought of her own mother, who lived in Ibradi with her sister. She worked in the city, sending her family what money she could. During the day Maryam was a nurse, but that made just enough money to cover her expenses. Extra work like waitressing was for her family. Someday she would marry and be able to bring her mother to live with her. Perhaps she would have a large house in the north of the city with a gate and rooms ready to be filled with children.

"I have no one. I am just a lonely old man taking kindness from a beautiful girl. Now get back to work before anyone notices how long you've been gone."

"You'll keep my secret won't you? I wouldn't want the devils to think I wasn't being respectful," she winked conspiratorially.

"If you'll keep mine."

The old man held up his hands to display the swollen knuckles that betrayed his age.

As Maryam returned to the party, the sounds of popular music wafted through the open door, assaulting the old man's ears. He sat lost in his thoughts of another young woman who had once fretted about his age.

Recai! There you are!" Darya exclaimed as she approached the low stool he had deposited himself on.

The entire party was aflame discussing the interloper, but no one asked him directly, no one would cross the line to say, "Are you the one? Have you returned?" Darya was full of excitement wanting to introduce the mysterious man to her benefactor. She was sure the Recai Osman she had spent the evening with was the son of Baris and Pinar. His death had rocked the city, but here before her was his flesh-and-blood ghost.

She had heard the story of Recai's parents and felt a kinship with him, even as a child. She remembered little about the time when her own father had been alive. In pictures and memories he always wore a bright smile. Darya's mother died in childbirth, and when she was only four months old her father married a Jewish woman against his family's wishes. They shunned him and left him to negotiate life without their loving support. Despite the difficulty, he loved his new wife very much and even had a child by her, a prized son.

The only family member who ever held the boy was Mahmet, the devoted brother and loving uncle. He was also the only one who had known, without a doubt, his brother's son had not been conceived within their marriage. When Darya's father died she was seven and her younger brother only four. Mahmet took her into his home to raise as his own, leaving the Jews out in the desert where they belonged.

He was an imposing figure at well over 180 centimeters, perhaps 185 or even 190. Mahmet managed to make Darya feel small and fragile, something she enjoyed only in his protective shadow. In addition to his height were the extra four-and-a-half or five stones hanging impressively from his frame, creating the impression he was larger than life, as big as a god or an ogre.

"Recai."

Darya said his name again, pulling his attention from the increasing number of onlookers following his movements. His eyes snapped to her and he stood abruptly. Her hand reached out and her fingers wrapped around his wrist.

"Come, come on, my uncle would like to meet the man who rescued me from the foyer!"

Darya was spinning from the excitement of the evening and her three glasses of champagne. All of her planning, all of her years of being unnoticed and ignored were paying off. Tonight she was beautiful and important. She spoke freely and men and women alike listened. Tonight she could exist in the world.

"Your uncle?"

"Yes! Mayor Yilmaz."

"Darya... Yilmaz?" he demanded.

"Yes...it's not a very common name."

Darya was unsure what to make of Recai's reaction. Her uncle was an influential man, the ruler of this small kingdom. If Recai was actually the son of Baris and Pinar, a meeting between him and her uncle should be something he sought, not something he avoided! But Recai didn't look right; his coloring and stance made Darya uneasy.

"Recai?"

"I don't know if it's a wise idea," Recai said, his face tight and hard as he spoke.

"I.... Did I do something wrong?"

"No, of course not! I...kahretsin!" He swore as he dragged a hand down his face, feeling the deep lines created by so many years in the sun.

"I'm sorry Darya, I..."

"It's all right."

She reached out again, placing her hand on his face, earning the disapproving glance of more than one of the party's patrons. She allowed her thumb to stroke his cheek along the faded scar.

"Thank you. I should go."

He stepped back, breaking the spell of her touch.

"Why?"

"I'm not… I wasn't invited."

"You were by me. And apparently an unescorted woman is in danger even at an event such as this."

Her eyes shone, but their light was lost in the black hole surrounding Recai.

"You never know what form danger may come in. Darya, this wasn't a good idea, I didn't think and…"

"You are Recai Osman?"

"I told you that."

"Yes, that's not a very common name in Elih, either."

"Not anymore."

"Your parents. They were Baris and Pinar Osman?" Darya ventured, finally asking the question on everyone's lips.

Sabiha Kaya was running late. She had been at her women's prayer group at Sister Aisha's house and lost track of time. The other women lived closer or had drivers who would come and get them when they were out after curfew, but Sabiha had nothing like that. All she had was her brother, Fahri, who was working late at some event downtown tonight.

Aisha had asked her to stay until Fahri got off duty and could come pick her up, or until her own father returned from his evening shift at work, but Sabiha knew Fahri would be far more angered by the inconvenience than the idea of his little sister walking home at night. No matter what dogma he may have spewed since he joined the RTK, Fahri was still the selfish bastard he had been since they were kids and Sabiha couldn't stand to miss class at the university again tomorrow due to whatever bruises her brother's discipline left on her face.

Above her the clouds gathered, pulling together reinforcements and awaiting their moment. The air came together with a violent crash. Thunder boomed in the atmosphere as miles beyond the city, the winds began to blow.

Aisha lived in a residential part of the city, about a twenty-five minute walk from the apartment complex Sabiha lived in. It was late enough that the roads would be mostly empty and dark—most people would be hurrying to their next location, not spending time scrutinizing one unescorted woman.

The small two-bedroom apartment she and her brother shared was above a halal market and next to the only movie theater in the city. It was loud. She never managed to get the smell of roasting flesh and popcorn out of the walls, but it was all Fahri could afford after paying for her tuition at the small women's college. She wanted to work, but her brother wouldn't have it, wanting her to finish her degree, get married, and get out of his hair as quickly as possible. These days it was impossible to find husbands for girls without a degree. Men of stature wanted wives who brought prestige to the union, even if they never intended to allow them to work. Having an educated wife had become a status symbol, but few men were interested in a liberated one. Fahri was determined to find Sabiha a solid match that would reflect well on him and maybe even elevate his own position, while she was happy to study her faith and feed her mind.

Darkness wrapped itself around her, a shadow hiding her within the city. A black hijab and denim overcoat concealed her skin from even the prying eyes of the honey-colored moon.

"...." Recai began, his mouth dry.

Before he had the opportunity to continue, his words were interrupted by a piercing ring. The sound of an alarm jarred the crowd, refocusing their minds on the danger that lived outside the boundaries of their homes. Elih might be a city, but it was still the desert. Descendants of Bedouins, Caucasians, and Arabs inhabited a city filled with ancient memories of the destruction sand could bring.

"Sand..." Darya whispered and grabbed hold of Recai's arm.

"What?" he shook his head, not understanding the impending danger. The alarm's shriek disoriented and confused him. There had been no sirens like this when he'd last been in the city.

"Come on. I live a few blocks from here; we can go there and not have to sit out the storm surrounded by the stench of all these people."

"A sandstorm?"

"Yes!"

She tugged his arm, pulling him toward the door. Recai responded to her desire to escape the hotel before the security gates came down, trapping everyone inside until the storm passed. Around them party-goers searched for their spouses or escorts, frantically debating if they could get to the safety of home or if they would be confined here. Voices rang out, calling above the alarm, hoping to be heard through the din of voices.

Taking his hand, Darya wove them through the scurrying crowd. Over the din the concierge announced: "A flash kum firtinasi is approaching the city. All attendees must remain calm and within the ballroom."

The staff frantically cleared plates and glasses, preparing themselves to spend the night in the back room of the hotel out of sight of the party-goers, who would be trapped within the hall.

A young woman and a slow-moving old man slid out the back door, praying to be faster than the encroaching sandstorm.

The hotel's warning siren accelerated, alerting people that the security gates would be closing over all windows and doors. Darya kicked off her heels and ducked through the crowd, rushing toward the entryway with Recai in tow. He moved without thought, allowing her to guide his body while his mind reeled.

Breaking through the clamor of bodies, Darya and Recai slipped out the entrance as the gates began to close. Outside, she turned toward him, the exhilaration of their escape animating her face.

"We made it!" she laughed, still holding his hand. The night heat was stifling and charged with electricity.

"My car…" Recai said, leading her down the street to where he had parked. Darya's elation was infectious, as she chattered excitedly.

"I wouldn't have been able to survive a night in there. Those people! Who would think the richest of them would be so stupid?"

"Darya!" Recai reprimanded with a smile as they approached the vehicle.

"Sycophants, all of them. Happy to follow my uncle so long as they're above the law. Who are the laws for, if not for those who think they're above them?"

Recai glanced above them and watched as the stars began to blot out one by one, the dense atmosphere moving in.

"Get in," he commanded as he opened the door for her.

"A please would be nice," she flirted, missing the tension in his voice.

To Darya this was simply another adventure, another diversion from her day-to-day life. Sandstorms weren't regular, but they weren't uncommon—nothing to become hysterical over.

Recai slid in the driver's side and fired to life what sounded like an enormous engine. They were moving almost immediately after she settled in her seat.

Speeding down the street, Recai kept both hands on the wheel.

"When did they start sounding alarms?"

"Two years ago. A number of people were caught in a sudden storm and died. My uncle implemented the warning system all over the city. I live up here on the corner," Darya pointed out.

The danger crept in on her as sirens in every section of the city blared. The winds picked up outside, a tell-tale sign that the storm would be on top of them soon. Rain evaporated in the heat above the city, leaving only the driving pressure and freeing the wind to rip through the world without restraint.

Darya sat in silence, watching out the window. The storm was coming quickly. *When they appear without warning like this the Kurds say it's the mountain sending its devils to punish the city.* Darya had always laughed at their ignorance, but wondered if tonight there might be some truth to their legends.

"Here," Darya indicated and Recai pulled in front of the tallest building in Elih: Çagdas Tower.

He opened his door and ran to the other side in time to help Darya onto the sidewalk. Street lights flickered and the wind whipped around them with increasing speed. The main streets became the most dangerous first, allowing the wind to pick up momentum without anything to slow its path; soon the wind itself would be almost as dangerous as the sand it brought.

The front door of the Çagdas Tower was unattended, the doorman likely hiding somewhere within the safety of the building far from the curved glass doors that welcomed all who lived within. The building was grand in design and size. Its impression was one of power and strength.

Recai rushed her to the entrance.

"Come in," Darya said when he slowed his pace.

"Darya, I shouldn't."

Stepping closer to him, she allowed her palms to rest on his chest.

"It's dangerous out here. You can't drive in this wind. There's no time. Come in."

A palm slid down an arm.

A sigh broke through the howl of the storm.

A hand was placed gently on a hip, pulling bodies closer until there was no room between them.

Recai slowly lowered his lips to Darya's, without hesitation.

The tires on Recai's Marussia B2 screamed as he pulled away from the stunned woman left standing outside her building. Her uncovered hair whipped around her face in the mounting cry of the incoming storm. No rain had fallen but the winds spoke of disaster.

Recai drove off into the fury of the mounting kum firtinasi. The silence of the night was blotted out with what seemed like the screams of devils, and the dead who accused him with their absence.

Abandoned us...

Forgot us...

Betrayed her...

Sand hung above the buildings, frozen in time as the storm gathered momentum, preparing for its assault. The orange night howled as Recai pushed his car faster toward the impending storm. He felt the gears shift and grind as they bore down to meet the demands he placed on the engine. The power at his hands filled him with a sense of freedom and as he sped faster—he longed more for escape.

Why had he done it? Why had he kissed a woman he barely knew? Recai had fought to change himself, to become the kind of man his mother would be proud of. The kind of man who could have saved Rebekah. But in the end he was still just a useless child, ruled by nothing but his own whims. How had he ever thought coming back to Elih would make a difference? That someone like him could replace his father?

He was a coward and he yearned for silence. He never found it in the desert, in his travels, in books, or even inside himself. All he wanted was to feel his loss with purity of mind.

The storm sped toward him, bringing sand and grit so sharp it could rip through a man's skin without sympathy. Before him a wall of yellow death loomed. The street ran haphazardly through the suburbs and stretched beyond the city into the desert where the wind was gathering strength. With nothing to slow its advance the kum firtinasi grew to astronomical heights, filling the sky with its rage.

Recai slammed on his breaks, burning off the outer layer of rubber on his tires. Faced with the power of the desert, his instinct to survive kicked in. He pulled the car around as soon as he regained traction and sped north toward his family home in the hills above the city. Behind him the banshee's cry dulled as he backtracked.

Once safely ahead of the storm, Recai slowed and sank into his seat, his hands shaking with adrenaline, his body exhausted. He drove on instinct, retracing the roads and neighborhoods he could name in his sleep, returning to the only real home he'd ever had, returning to his isolation.

The bile of his failure rose in his mouth, bringing tears to his eyes. Rebekah's eyes flashed before him as the desert song rang out above.

There's no escape from the guilt of doing nothing. All I have now is the gripping pain that haunts me even in my dreams.

Every night for years Recai had dreamed of his mother. Now the faces of two women he loved and had been unable to save blurred and combined, creating a ghost more ghastly than any movie maker's imagination.

"*No!*" A voice called out in the eerily lit night. The cry was soft but it penetrated the air, pierced through his darkly tinted windows and directly into Recai.

Looking in the rear view mirror, Recai saw the storm looming in the distance, moving steadily closer like some army of vengeful angels come to consume the world.

The soft voice broke through anew: "*Alla'humma ajirni!*"

The plea was quiet, yet deafening to Recai.

Sand caused the wheels of the powerful car to slip, breaking traction and forcing Recai's hand. The vehicle slid sideways along the street, the momentum slamming it against the back of a parked car.

The impact of the vehicles ripped metal against metal. Glass rained down on him as he fought the airbag for breath. The passenger's side was crushed inward. The frame on the driver's side was bent so that Recai's arm was caught and pinched beneath its strength. Recai's circulation slowed, and gradually he lost the ability to feel his fingers. The drowning sound of the incoming storm faded behind the pounding of his struggling pulse. Thinking this may finally be the end of his regret and pain, Recai closed his eyes in submission to Allah's will. He welcomed the blissful unconsciousness.

Before him the image of Rebekah stood in his mind, beautiful in her house-dress and gently draped hijab. An afterlife in her arms would be heaven enough for the beaten heart of a man who had seen nothing but cruelty and pain. As she reached out for him, he heard it again.

"*No, please!*"

Aman. A voice. Darkness tangled her thoughts with fear and childhood warnings.

Sabiha, you shouldn't be walking alone, she'd heard it say.

Stupidity had made her rash; selfish concerns about her brother caused her to make the worst possible mistake—the kind of mistake that would make her wish she had died, if by any chance she managed to survive.

The low voice knew her name, knew her family name—it had come specifically for her.

She ignored its call, quickening her pace. A laugh broke out in the night, mocking her fear. Suddenly the owner of the voice grabbed her, turning her around to face him.

Refusing to meet the voice's gaze, Sabiha fixed her eyes forward. Her gaze came to rest on his arm where she saw the outline of a tattoo, dark and menacing. A snake's tail circled his bicep and disappeared behind his back, only to reveal itself on the other side of his neck with two onyx eyes staring at her, unblinking.

What kind of man cannot die?

Pain was inconsequential to Recai when Heaven once again refused his entry. Wrenching his arm out of its trap, Recai slammed his shoulder against the dash. Glass fell around him again at the same moment the airborne sand arrived. The wind was warm as it swirled within the demolished car. He crawled out into the sting of sand against his fresh wounds, cleansing his mind.

"*No*," the voice called again. "*Help me*!"

Grit and particles swam around Recai, spinning his mind and swirling in the air around his feet as it rose and enveloped him in its cruelty. Quickly he tore off his bloody shirt and pulled it over his face, covering his mouth and nose like a niqab. He tied the sleeves tightly around his head so the shirt clung to his skin, blocking the suffocating sand from entering his lungs.

An eerie glow came over the city as the light that shone from the lamps above and through the windows of apartments lit up each grain of sand. The movement of the air swept Recai's hair back from his face, revealing the scars in his hairline and forcing his eyes into a sharp and fearsome glare.

Following the voice that called to him from beyond the wail of the desert, Recai strode into the opaqueness before him. The sand parted, swirling in the air, and closed behind him again as he passed through the street and into the alley from which the sounds of terror rang out like a siren.

The grating sound of the sand hurtling through the city created a howling reverberation between the buildings. Within the alley Recai was protected from its ferocity, but particles crept in slowly, like a river overflowing. He saw a woman lying crumpled on the ground. A man in a tank top and jeans stood above her.

Though he knew the man before him had been cruel, the extent of his sin was unimportant to Recai. All he knew was there was a woman, alone and afraid, covered in blood with her denim abaya ripped open. Recai's mind flashed from the image of his mother standing rigid in the night, to the cruel murder of Rebekah, to the woman before him—and as an angel of death he leaped forward to avenge them all.

Before he was seen by his target Recai struck, knocking the man against the concrete wall. Wind gusted around them, blowing sand in from the main streets, which slithered along the ground. It whipped around them as Recai's fury grew.

He swung again, but the man jerked out of the way. Recai stumbled forward before he ducked and lashed out. Pulling on years of wrestling and military training, his movements were smooth and unpredictable. He struck out with arms, elbows, and feet, making it impossible to anticipate where his next blow would land.

Taking a boxing stance, the woman's attacker stood his ground despite the blood spilling from his nose and the swelling of his knee. Sand obscured his vision and saturated the air he breathed, but the man would not look away. Above them the storm thundered and the rain at last began to fall. Sand and rain competed for dominance over the city, falling and flying with such ferocity that the sting of it against the skin felt like a thousand tiny shards of glass.

Thick, hot ozone filled Recai's lungs, choking his humanity.

The men lunged at each other, falling in the wet silt that shifted beneath their feet with every step. Recai kicked the man's knee, bending it backwards, causing him to cry out and fall to the ground.

The man looked up, his face distorted in a snarl of hatred. Recai watched as he struggled to stand. With a grunt of pain the man finally stood upright before him, allowing Recai to take in his full appearance for the first time.

The snake.

Recai's hold on sanity shattered as he peered into the same two black eyes that had mocked him as Rebekah lay bleeding across his lap.

A scream rose into the night, competing with the sky for the very ear of God.

PART 3

"IF YOU BRING FORTH WHAT IS WITHIN YOU, WHAT YOU
BRING FORTH WILL SAVE YOU. IF YOU DO NOT BRING FORTH
WHAT IS WITHIN YOU, WHAT YOU DO NOT BRING
FORTH WILL DESTROY YOU."

The Gospel of St. Thomas (Dead Sea Scrolls) verse 70

How is he?" Maryam asked cautiously, sticking her head into the small concrete room.

In a moment of charity she had invited the aged bartender back to her small apartment when she saw him fleeing the hotel despite the looming kum firtinasi. The floor in the building she lived in was designated for women only, but what harm could there be in sheltering an old man in the basement utility room during a storm?

The main entrance had been locked and barricaded against the looting that sometimes occurred in the aftermath of a storm such as this, so Maryam and the bartender had walked from the hotel to the small alley her apartment backed up against, where a maintenance door allowed access to her building to either descend to the basement or head up to the floors full of rooms rented by the week.

With a sigh the old man looked up at her and responded, "Sleeping now. Lunatic clamored around up there and screamed most of the night. I don't understand how no one heard."

"I told you no one lives above the utility room; it's just a grocery up there. No one was even there last night."

Maryam pushed the heavy door open the rest of the way with her hip and set the tray she had brought on an orphaned box sitting lonely in the middle of the room. The room was stuffy, full of the building's inner workings: hot water heater, AC unit, electrical box. Tools were placed haphazardly on shelves lining the wall next to her. The air conditioner's humidifier attachment wheezed as it leaked cool water, which evaporated before the fluid even reached the ground.

Maryam sat on the dusty floor, avoiding the obvious stains. She pulled her abaya over her legs and eyed the large metal door hidden in the darkness at the far end of the room. The locked storage closet, which was used by the building manager to store tools and other valuable items, had become a prison for the berserker they had found the night before.

She was glad to be back in her own clothes instead of the blouse and long skirt that had served as her uniform at yesterday's event. As a single woman living alone in the city, Maryam found more than enough reasons to adhere to wearing a hijab; without it she felt she might as well have been walking through the crowd naked, her ears and neck cold against the open air. Some days she resisted covering, but in the end she always found comfort and strength beneath her scarf.

"Effendi…"

"No, I am not. Stop calling me that. I'm not owed your respect, I'm just a stupid old man," Hasad shook his head wearily. "I owe you an explanation. You invited me to your home so I wouldn't be stuck in that hotel during the storm, and instead of thanks I gave you a big festering boil of trouble."

"Not how I would have phrased it but, yes, you did."

Maryam smiled. Something about Hasad calmed her and even made her trust him, though they'd just met. Her father died when she was a teenager, leaving her at the mercy of her five older brothers. Her sister, the eldest, had already married by then. Having been raised more by her brothers than her mother Maryam learned that a bit of rough talk didn't equate to a rough soul.

"Effendi, the man we found last night, you recognized him."

"I did, I do. He's not someone I ever expected to see again, but I can't say it's an unwelcome surprise."

"He was going to kill that man. When we found him in the alley, there was so much blood! Why did you save him? Why leave the other out in the storm?"

"I don't have answers about what happened. We'll have to wait and hear it from him, but I have no doubt that whatever happened, Recai was only protecting that woman."

"Sabiha..." Maryam murmured.

"Was that her name?"

Hasad's face softened. Staring down at the dirty concrete floor he wrung his hands.

"Yes, she's gone home now."

"Did she tell you what happened?"

"No; she only told me her name, then she fell asleep as soon as I got her to my room. When I woke up she was on the phone with someone. I think her father or brother. Someone was going to meet her and take her home."

He stood suddenly, panic evident on his face.

"Do they know where we are?"

"She was going to meet him in the tea house across the street. But, obviously, she knows where I live."

"No, I mean, does anyone know I'm down here? That he's down here?" asked Hasad, jerking his head toward the closet where Recai was hidden.

"*Effendi, w*hat is going on?"

She looked up and stared hard at the old man. The beating they had broken up last night; the man they had pulled inside, crying and screaming as they went; the girl who had come so near to being another in a long tradition of ruined women—it all proved to be more than she could process.

"My full name is Hasad Sofear and three years ago my daughter..."

His voice cracked as he pushed out the name sitting lodged in his throat.

"...Rebekah... my daughter Rebekah was killed."

Maryam blinked in surprise and pulled her *abaya* over her feet, seeking the security of her covering to keep her strong.

"Did he . . . ?!" Maryam exclaimed, instantly assuming the bloody man with the vicious eyes locked in the closet more than capable of such an act.

"No, the RTK, they killed him, too…or they tried."

Hasad held out his hands, uncurling them painfully to show the striated scars along his flesh, all the way up to his elbows.

"When I got there she had been… she was dead already…there was a fire…"

"I'm sorry."

"The things they had done to her…she was gone and the man locked in there was lying with her, close to death, protecting her body with what strength he had."

"Inna lillahi wa inna ilahi raji'un," she whispered against the horror of the world. Man was perhaps a worse threat to humanity's soul than any devil.

"He was bleeding and unconscious and the house was on fire. The sirens hadn't sounded yet and everyone was still asleep. For anyone to find them, wrapped around each other… What a disgrace it would have been!"

Hasad folded his hands one over the other and stood up. He looked at the metal door that locked Recai safely away. It stood in silent judgment.

"I should have helped him. I should have made sure he survived. Instead I dragged him outside, lifted him onto my camel and left him in the desert with my water canteen. It was the best I could do by him then; I had to get back to Rebekah. When I returned to the house the fire had consumed everything. I never knew what happened to him. I always assumed he survived and returned to his world. When I recognized him at the party—"

"He was there? At the hotel?" Maryam interrupted in surprise. Her eyes watched him. She was like a child listening to a ghost story, mesmerized but unable to turn away.

"He was there. He didn't recognize me, but I knew him. The scar on his cheek was fresh and raw when I first met him, and the hue of his beard is easy to recognize."

"Laa ela-ha el-lal-la," she prayed softly to herself, closing her eyes and shaking her head.

"Last night he was one of them…" Hasad continued.

"When we found him in the alley, he was *not* one of them."

"No. I don't imagine he ever will be."

Siktir lan," he swore, spitting out thick, dried blood that had mixed with the sand in his mouth.

The pain in Isik Mosafir's head was rivaled only by the intense throbbing of his leg. Looking down, he half expected it to be gone; amputation being the only thing he was able to think of that could cause so much pain.

"Who was that got veren mother-fucker?"

Reaching out, Isik grabbed the edge of a dumpster and pulled himself up. His knee couldn't bear weight, but he was determined to get back home before anyone found him here. The last thing he needed was to be questioned by the RTK.

He'd left them a few years back and had been able to stay under the radar thanks to the friends he still had in the ranks. He also spent most of his time doing errands for the right people, people he knew by being kin to some of those same *right* people. But now his clothes were saturated with blood and he could barely walk; no way he'd get away without having to answer some questions.

What is your name?
Who is your family?
Isik snorted. *Who, indeed?*

Blood had dried on the ground around him into the remnants of last night's sandstorm. The oozing red congealed with dry particles to create a gory landscape. Isik wondered how much had come from his body. Overhead the sky was dark and threatening, the air thick as a rainstorm moved in.

The rain would keep the sand down for now. Rain after a kum firtinasi was a mixed blessing. Isik needed to get inside before the silt under his feet turned to sludge and made walking even more treacherous.

Carefully, Isik placed one foot in front of the other, leaning against the dumpster and then the wall for support. He noticed the bloodstain on the cement where he had thrown his attacker from last night, and the empty spot where Sabiha's body should have been.

The memory was too confusing. He couldn't wrap his mind around what had happened. It didn't make any sense. Who would have come after him like that over some whore walking at night alone? Who would care enough to take him on? And, most concerning, who would be strong enough to have beaten him this severely?

He'd only been carrying out his order—to make the sister of RTK officer Fahri Kaya pay for his offense against Darya the night before. That's the way it was. Women paid for everything; they were the evil at the core of a rotten apple.

His whole life, Isik had fought for everything he had. Son of a Turk whose family had disowned him for marrying a Jewish woman; he was the dirty little secret of his extended family, but he made sure they would never brush him under the rug like they had his father. Once he was old enough to walk he started studying Karakucak, the Turkish form of wrestling, and he would grapple with the neighborhood boys. When they were old enough to learn they shouldn't be friends with a Jew, especially one whose father died and whose mother lived alone, he was already bigger and stronger than they were and he made sure they knew it. He fought to stay alive, he fought to defend his father, and he fought to prove who he was. He was still fighting.

Today, he fought against the nausea threatening to take over as he hobbled to the end of the alley where he had hidden his car.

The concrete floor was cold. Below ground the temperature is the same everywhere—an even 10 degrees Celsius—even in Elih, where the sun beats down with a relentless heat. A shiver shot up Recai's spine, shaking him awake. He was slow to open his eyes, his mind still blurry.

Where am I? What...

He looked down to check his watch and found it gone, as was, to his surprise, his shirt. His tuxedo pants were ripped at the knees, but other than a few aches he did not feel too badly injured. It was too dark to check and see what surface damage had been done. Recai reached up and touched his face, wincing at the contact. His memory was fuzzy from the previous night. Looking back in his memory, he saw only swirling cyclones of sand.

Across the room a sliver of light shone from under what must have been the door. Recai heard voices coming from the other side but couldn't make out what they were saying.

Slowly, he used the dim glow to take in his surroundings. The room was dark and small. There had been shelves along the wall at one point but someone, or something, had ripped them from their posts. Packages of paper towels and disinfectant were sprawled about the floor.

He pulled himself up to his knees, hissing through his teeth at the pain of concrete grating against raw flesh. Tiny pieces of ancient dirt and grime worked themselves into his wounds, intermingling with his bloodstream. With cautious movements, he felt his way along the floor in the dim light to the door. As he approached, the voices became clear in spite of their hushed tones: a man and a woman.

Why am I here?

He dizzily relaxed back down on the ground, allowing his head to rest on the floor's welcome coolness.

The darkness was seductive, the lure of sleep difficult to resist. The voices beyond the door spoke just beneath the level of his understanding. He deciphered the familiar tones of Turkish and Arabic intermixed so completely they had to be of someone from the city. The second voice was lower and softer, speaking in an unfamiliar cadence. Soothing, like a chant. Recai had heard this accent before but could not place it. His ears strained for a clearer sound.

As he lay in the dark cellar, his memories swirled like the storm he had been caught in: the voices from outside, flashes of a woman beaten and afraid. As he moved farther from sleep a final image broke through—a man, snarling in the storm, with a snake tattoo winding up his arm and peeking out from behind his neck.

Recai bolted upright and burst to his feet, the previous night's events overwhelming him as they flooded back. The man with the tattoo…the snake's eyes…. Rebekah's death rose to the forefront of his mind as the man's face shone in his memory.

Outside this little room was someone who was keeping him in here. Whoever had pulled him off the tattooed man had dragged him down here. His rage-filled memory told him that much. Last night, with Darya, he had momentarily allowed himself to forget his pain. But all he accomplished was adding more confusion to his chaotic heart. His need for revenge raged anew.

"Open this door!" Recai roared. Mustering what strength he had he threw himself against the metal keeping him inside the concrete cage. His shoulder burned from the impact but he didn't stop his assault.

"Let me *out*! Who put me in here? Open this door or—"

"If you were calm I'd feel a lot better about opening the door," a smooth voice said in a familiar cadence.

"I'd be calm if I wasn't locked in this hell hole. Open!"

"Ah, and there's the downward spiral. I cannot let you out until you are calm, and you cannot be calm until you are out. It seems we are at a bit of an impasse, eh, Recai?"

Recai was still. For a moment he just stood there in his cell and stared in wonderment at the door. How had this person outside known his name? His confusion was so complete his anger dissipated. The attendees of the mayor's party and Darya knew his identity, but no others, and they were all still under lock and key from the storm.

A quiet shuffling from outside pulled him back to his current predicament. A click echoed through the small room, ricocheting off of every surface as his captor unlocked and opened the door.

Light flooded in, momentarily blinding Recai, forcing him to squint and move away from the open door that offered him freedom. As his eyes adjusted, his anger returned. The silhouetted form before him was outlined with florescent light.

"You locked me in here, you kidnapped me," he seethed, crouching down in preparation to attack.

"No, Son, I protected you."

The familiar voice washed over him. *Son.* No one had called him that in a very long time. The name soothed him somewhat, and piqued his curiosity.

"How do you know me?"

His voice shook as he held back his instinct to burst out into the light beyond his warden.

"You knew me once. You knew my daughter…"

The husky voice drifted off, leaving Recai feeling alone and cold. As Recai took a step forward the man retreated into the main room, allowing the light to illuminate his wizened face and tired eyes.

"You knew Rebekah…"

Recai's gut wrenched as if he had been hit. His eyes watered—the image of her calling him to heaven, then leaving him earthbound and alone returned. His emotions fought for voice, but there were none which could convey his shock as the accent of the man before him suddenly made perfect sense.

"Hasad?"

Recai reached out and stepped toward the old man as if seeing a ghost.

"How…?"

The pain in his gut twisted its way through Recai, wringing every drop of misery out of him, spilling it on the floor, leaving him to wade in its sea.

"Son, are you all right?"

Hasad's gruff exterior fell away as he took in the broken young man before him.

Recai's eyes filled with water again as he fell on his knees before the old man. His life had been saved so many years before, only to be the cause of Rebekah's death. There was nothing about him that was worth saving. He failed time and again, never able to do or be enough. But he ached for the understanding of the only soul who knew the pain he suffered. He wept for the first time in a long time since Rebekah's death. Hasad placed forgiving hand on his shoulder.

"Hasad, I'm so sorry. I should have… I should have protected her. I shouldn't have lived when she didn't." Recai's voice cracked as the tears streamed down his face, cleaning a path through his bloody features. "I could have—"

"There's nothing anyone could have done."

Hasad did not embrace Recai, nor did he move away. He simply stood, accepting the other's tears with a strength he didn't possess, but which Recai needed.

"I don't know why I lived. I never wanted to. I failed her in this life, I would have been happy to follow her into the next."

"Recai," Hasad began, pulling Recai's attention up out of his misery. "I pulled you from that fire. There's a reason you lived. There's a reason you're here. Stand up."

Hasad waited patiently as Recai stood and once again took in the old man before him. Hasad hadn't changed much since Recai last saw him in Çayustu. The lines in his face were deeper and his skin looser, but wild intelligence still shone from his eyes.

Those eyes bore into Recai as he asked, "Now, where have you been?"

Darya sat in front of her vanity with a soft smile on her face. The celebration for her uncle had ended unexpectedly, and while she was frustrated with Recai's rejection, she didn't take it to heart.

Her long hair hung down her back over her silk nightgown as she poured a small amount of oil into her hands. She rubbed them together filling the room with the earthy scent of sandalwood, transforming the heat from oppressive to languid.

It had been three days since the kum fırtinasi, and the sand was still settling into the cracks of the streets. Another week would pass before the reddish tint would be gone and life would return to normal. Until then she would stay in her apartment, thankful for the luxury of technology that allowed her to continue her work running the empire that funded her uncle's government.

She never knew where his funds came from and never asked; she simply invested and managed them, increasing his wealth exponentially. All the while she siphoned off just enough to run her own projects without anyone ever suspecting.

This morning her mind would not focus on business or on the constant insult of having to hide her face and name from those she worked with, enraging both her vanity and pride. Instead, her mind drifted to Recai. His lips had been soft and his hand sure when he placed it on her back to dance. When they spoke he had not avoided her eyes or acted as if she committed a sin by speaking her mind. He had laughed, and looked at her the way she dreamed someone would.

Whatever the reason he left, she didn't care. His momentary lapse in piety gave Darya a glimpse into the passionate man within.

Darya began to oil her hair. She moved section by section, applying moisture to her damaged strands, bringing back the beauty the desert heat had stolen. Pulling her hands along the length of her locks she weaved her fingers into her hair, spreading the oil evenly from scalp to ends. The process was time consuming but soothing, allowing her mind to drift.

While she worked, she closed her eyes and dreamt of a life with a man she hardly knew, a man with rare and insightful green eyes.

Darya prided herself on being capable. She ran her own life and made her own decisions, but something about a mate and equal appealed to her. She would give anything to have love. Real love—not the kind traded for favors or blackmail. The kind that freed you. She believed Recai was different from other men, that he would be able to appreciate all that she could offer.

In the hall she heard her attendants fuss about something. There was always a fuss about something. Her uncle insisted she have guards even in her own home, keeping her in purdah regardless of his claims to value her above all his other confidants. She held the reins of his power, yet had none of her own.

She longed for change, for freedom. Her gilded cage closed in around her every day. The constraints so tight she feared she may run out of space completely. She grew tired of being allowed out in the street only if she covered herself. She resented being permitted to work only if she hid behind false names and computers. Someday the whole city would know who spoke directly into the mayor's ear, and then she could take what she was due.

Bursting through the doors to her bedroom, her housekeeper struggled to keep someone out.

"You can't simply walk in there! This is her *bedroom!*"

"It's fine," Darya stated calmly upon seeing her half-brother's silhouette. She turned on her ottoman to face the disruption.

"*Beyan!*" the housekeeper protested.

"I said it's fine."

"Your uncle would not be happy," Darya's housekeeper said with a *tsk* before eyeing the man now standing just inside the double doors leading to Darya's suite.

"Sister…" he began as the housekeeper slid past him and shut the doors behind her.

"Why are you here?" Darya demanded, annoyed by his presence in her home. Their relationship was not supposed to be public; that's what made it work so well. As soon as anyone associated them with each other, or found out they were related, so many of Darya's plans would be compromised.

"Don't start with me! Do you see these fucking bruises on my face?"

"So? You're always doing something insane. It's about time someone raised a hand to you," Darya responded blithely to her half-brother's harsh tone. She turned back to her vanity, watching him in the reflection as she poured more oil into her hand to resume her task.

"It was your dirty errand that did this, *Sister,*" he sneered, his eyes narrowing in the mirror until the left one disappeared under the swelling of his brow. He resembled his mother so much it was hard to believe he was her father's child; but Darya remembered the wedding and his birth in painfully vivid detail, despite having been only four years old when he was born.

"Is that so? Fahri Kaya's little sister was more than you could handle?"

Isik stalked toward his sister with a heavy limp. As he approached, his façade never softened and his eyes never moved away from hers. When he was behind her he took her hair in his hands and combed the oil through it with calloused fingers. Darya tensed, unsure of what to make of this seemingly affectionate gesture.

"That little bitch wasn't the issue. She barely put up a fight."

His voice was smooth and deep.

"Not surprising, they rarely do."

Darya allowed her mind and body to relax into her half-brother's ministrations.

"There was someone else there."

"In the kum firtinasi? There was someone else out in that storm? I thought only you and the devil were brave enough for that," Darya mocked, knowing Isik's penchant for exaggeration. Maybe that girl really had been too much for him.

"Darya, I'm not in the mood for your shit."

He yanked her hair back, forcing her to open her eyes and look up at him. She let out a small gasp at the assault before smiling up at him mischievously.

"There was someone out there!" Isik declared.

He held her still for a moment, his eyes boring into her, the threat of his presence palpable between them. Finally he released her and sat heavily on the end of her bed, stretching his injured leg out beside him. He was lucky it had only been dislocated and not broken by the dervish who attacked him.

Sighing, Isik brought his hands to his eyes, intending to rub the heels of his palms into his sockets to clear the confusion of his mind. He winced at the contact, his bruises still too raw.

Darya turned finally and leaned forward. Her nightgown fell apart slightly and allowed Isik a haram glimpse of skin.

"Look at me," he sighed, gesturing to his swollen face, his eyes softer than they had been in years.

Taken aback by Isik's momentary vulnerability she found herself reaching out to him.

"Tell me what happened…"

"I got your call and tracked down Kaya's sister," Isik smiled, re-donning his mask and allowing himself another glance at his half-sister's cleavage. "You know I love it when you get vengeful."

"It does look good on me," she flirted, resuming the game before sitting back and covering herself.

"I found her at some house over in Yesiltepe. I watched, hoping she would get a car and I could catch her at home alone, but she decided to walk."

"Masha'Allah!" Darya clapped and leaned back.

"Stupid bitch walked through the city in the middle of a sandstorm! I drove ahead and parked, waiting for her to get near her home so Fahri wouldn't have to search too far for her. Everything went smooth, and then…fuck, Darya…"

"What?"

"I… I really don't know…. Some *thing* came out of the street, the sand all up in the air. I could hardly see with the storm moving in but it was spinning all around him.. He disappeared in it and then he was right in front of me."

Darya narrowed her eyes, trying to follow her brother's disjointed thoughts.

"He fought, was a good fighter, but that wasn't it. He…he had something over his face and I couldn't see him right, the storm caught up to us and…"

Darya stood up, disturbed by his loss for words. She stepped toward Isik and tenderly placed her hand on his shoulder. At her touch he wrenched away and struggled until he stood on his feet, towering over her.

"Don't pity me! It was that sandstorm. It did something to him."

Isik began pacing the room, the pain in his knee forgotten as his confusion and insult raged. As he walked his anger grew until it threatened to overtake what reason he possessed.

"What are you talking about?" Darya asked.

"I'm telling you, there was something not right about that man. He came out of nowhere and was gone just as fast, leaving me there in the storm."

As she listened, Darya sat and watched Isik run his hands through his cropped hair in frustration. She had never seen him so unsettled.

"When I woke up, the girl was gone and the sand was covered in blood. I don't know…"

"She's safe?"

"I told you, someone attacked me."

Isik stopped his movement and stared at his sister.

"So you didn't finish your task?" she berated.

"He interrupted me!"

"Does she know who you are? Do any of them know who you are?"

"Does anyone what!?"

"Isik! Can this man track you back to me?"

"That's what it's about again." He continued pacing once more, the tight-fitting shirt he wore rolling with his shoulders as he seethed. "You aren't concerned that Sabiha is going to be able to describe me or that whoever the fuck was out there was able to do this in the first place?" He gestured angrily to his bruised and disfigured face.

"I am, but…"

"No, you're only concerned with it being connected to you. You selfish bitch!"

"No," Darya backtracked, standing cautiously, trying to calm her brother. "I was only... If anyone connected you to Mahmet..."

"Right, our beloved uncle," he hissed, the head of his tattoo peeking up out of his shirt, the snake tracking her with its eyes.

"Tell me about the man again, maybe...maybe there's something we can do to find him before he finds out who you are."

"And when we find him, I'm going to shit in his mouth and make him eat it before I take him apart, one piece at a time."

When Maryam read the headline in the paper, she knew instantly it was Recai. She recognized the line of his brow and the conflicted glower in his eyes in the picture.

Returning home from her shift at the hospital, she had stopped at the grocery beneath her apartment to buy eggs, rice, and juice, and maybe one of the cheap novels they kept behind the counter. If Abdullah was working, he would sneak her one of the novels restricted from women in the city. She hated breaking the rules, but nothing in her faith stopped her from expanding her mind. Those were the laws of men, and her life was governed by the laws of Allah.

As she stepped up to the counter, she placed her items and small canvas grocery bag next to the register. While Abdullah packed her items, she read over the headlines of the various newspapers, *Hurriyet*, *AGOS* and *Elih Gazetesi*. Next to the headline of the last paper appeared a sketch of a man

PARVATI K TYLER

wearing a niqab with narrow violent eyes. She stared at the image, mouth agape.

"Assalaamu alum Sister Maryam," Abdullah greeted.

"Walaikum as salaam," she replied automatically, eyes still glued to the paper.

"Amazing isn't it?"

"What?" Maryam lifted her eyes to the man behind the counter, having momentarily forgotten where she was. "Oh, yes, yes, amazing…"

"A woman was being attacked during the kum firtinasi and someone rescued her. They're calling him The SandStorm. She didn't get a good look at the man who saved her, but that's what they think he looks like."

Abdullah leaned across the counter, his long curly hair bouncing as he spoke, giving him the look of an over-friendly cocker-spaniel.

"Rescued her…" Maryam repeated

"The Holy Prophet, Salla Allahu 'Alaihi Wa Sallam, taught us it is the man's duty to protect women."

"He did…"

Maryam's thoughts were distracted. The image of the man on the paper glared out at the world as if he might set it aflame. She reached out and allowed her finger to trace over the headline: "Masked Protector Saves Woman from Ruin." Yes, the ruin would certainly have been the victim's, not that of the man who attacked her or the society that made it impossible for her to be outside of her home alone. No, the woman who was attacked would be the one forever ruined.

"Maryam, I would protect you."

Abdullah spoke quietly enough so that no one could overhear, even though no one else was in the small shop save the two. Maryam blushed and lowered her eyes, wishing she had worn one of her abayas instead of being seen in dirty scrubs.

"I worry about you living upstairs alone, traveling to the hospital every day."

"I have a car, I park safely, Abdullah. You needn't worry over me."

"I… want to worry over you…"

Maryam ducked her head lower and turned away from him slightly. Abdullah was a kind man. She enjoyed talking to him, but no flame of desire burned for him within her. However, his moment of softness allowed her a rare opportunity.

"Abdullah," she began her voice quiet and low, hoping not to inspire lust. "Do you think… could I have an *Elih Gazetesi?* This story, it's something I'd like to read."

Keeping her eyes down, Maryam held her breath, hoping the rules might be broken, just this once. Usually when she acquired something forbidden he offered it; she had never before asked.

"The mayor says allowing women to read the news is haram," Abdullah said, his voice unsteady.

"I'm not familiar with that hadith."

She was venturing into dangerous territory, and kept her eyes downcast, her stance modest and deferential. Waiting for his reply, her fingers itched to take the newspaper from its stand.

After a moment of silence she took twenty-five Turkish liras out of her bag and handed them to him, the silence between them threatening to burst into a scream. Normally she ignored the restrictions of the RTK and went her own way, living the life of a proper muslimah and staying out of trouble. This afternoon, in the stuffy heat of a small corner grocery, the reality of her oppression closed in on her.

Abdullah handed over her change and lingered, looking at her soft features. Before he allowed himself to over-think the consequences of his actions, he shoved a copy of the paper into her bag.

Two weeks later a small man sat uncomfortably on an oversized couch in the Osman estate's formal living room.

"I'm sorry, Recai, but I simply can't explain it," he repeated. The bright green of the room made his brown skin appear jaundiced. Or perhaps his sickly appearance was due to the fact that he could not explain a significant discrepancy in the corporation's books.

"You can't explain losing four *billion* dollars?" Recai pressed.

Recai sat rigid in his father's leather chair. His fists clenched and unclenched as his jaw strained. His body wanted to act, to beat an explanation out of Ali, the man in front of him, to force things to make sense. But his mind restrained him, locking him in place. His father would not have reacted so extremely, and Recai had a legacy to uphold.

Ali Kalkan had worked for the Osman Corporation for twenty years. He had advised Baris before his disappearance and had worked to keep the business running smoothly in the face of Baris's—then Recai's—sudden absences. Ali had always hoped that one day Baris would return. He never had much faith Recai could run things as he should.

Recai fumed and looked around the room. The familiar pain of a young boy's loss saturated the air, like everything in the home. His mother's linens shone brightly, reminding him of his solitude, and the décor remained a beautiful reminder of his misery. Recai's time at home was always painful but he could not bring himself to change anything. A portrait of his mother hung on the wall behind Kalkan's head, dwarfing him, her kind wisdom looking down on them.

"The books are in order, everything adds up, but in the end the numbers are short."

Kalkan studied his laptop intensely, hoping to find a miracle on the screen before him.

"There has to be an explanation, Ali. Money doesn't simply disappear." Recai closed his eyes in an attempt to calm himself. Nothing would come from him lashing out at Ali. The one thing he'd learned living in the desert was that only a clear mind could lead the way toward understanding.

"Your trust is still in good standing," Ali continued, hoping to appease the raging fire behind Recai's eyes. His return made as little sense as his sudden interest in the family business. His young employer had lived too many years overseas to know what was going on. And when he did return he was allowed freedoms others were denied, simply due to his name. How could he possibly understand what life was like in Elih? Ali couldn't afford to be fired or have his reputation tarnished by a rash boy playing at being a businessman.

But when called, Ali had no choice but to answer.

"That's what you think this is about? Money for me?" Recai seethed and paced along the length of the room.

The tall windows blazed with the glare of the late afternoon sun in the distance. No other homes had been built at this end of *Aydinkonak*. The nearest houses lined the opulent streets that stopped half a mile before reaching the Osman compound.

Outside the window nothing but the lush, irrigated lawn spanned before him. Recai was rich not only in lira but also in water. That lawn used more water than some communities were allotted in a week. Beyond it there was only desert until to the next city. The estate was isolated at the edge of the city, offering a view of the skyline from one side and open space from the other.

"Son…" Ali began, but swallowed his words when Recai turned on him, frustration burning in his eyes.

"The ex…executive committee hasn't changed in years," Ali stuttered, "and the Board of Directors is essentially the same as when your father ran things."

"Essentially?"

Recai ran a hand over his face, forcing himself to calm his heart. Anger only led to more anger. He needed to rein himself in.

"There's only been one new member in the last six years. Umm…" Ali scanned his document folder, looking for the most recent roster of the Board of Directors. "Dayar Yildirim," he pronounced proudly, happy to have at least one answer within his possession.

"Yildirim hasn't attended any meetings, though, and has always voted by proxy. I don't believe there is any issue with him," Ali continued.

The fan overhead moved the air in wide slow circles, creating a soft hum in the background of the conversation.

"Then what has happened? The profits remain high, rise higher every year, and the books show a profit, but the money is missing!"

"Yes…" Ali conceded.

"I want a full audit of the last five years." Recai turned to Ali and found his mouth open wide, shocked at the enormity of the project.

"I don't care who you have to hire or what you need to do, but this is a project for me directly. Do not report your findings to the executive committee or the Board. I want everything to come straight to me. And I want you to do it personally."

"Personally?"

"Yes. Ali, whatever is going on, we can't trust that others aren't involved. You knew my father. I know you aren't involved in this, but I need you to figure it out for me."

"I… I will find it." Ali's voice was soft, his emotions touched by Recai's sudden display of leadership and faith.

"Have we been giving out more loans?"

"No, the loans stopped soon after you… left."

Ali looked away, not wishing to bring up the subject of Recai's return. While mysterious, it was not out of the realm of possibility for a man of Recai's wealth and liberal views to simply decide to leave Elih for lands less conservative. Ali had known men in his youth who had done the same, left their country to study abroad and indulge in transgressions forbidden by their faith: sex, drinking, and sometimes worse. What was important was that they returned.

Recai sat back down and nodded, staring out the window again.

"I want the loans reinstated."

"The Board voted…" Ali faltered, the determination in the young man's eyes so much like his father's.

"I don't care what the Board voted." Recai's voice was steady. "Just do it, and tell anyone who questions you that it was directed by me personally."

"Bey Osman," a soft voice interrupted his thoughts. His attendant, Tamar, stood demurely in the arched doorway separating the living room from the foyer. "Would you and your guest care for something to drink?"

"No, Tamar, Ali will be leaving now."

Recai stood and walked out of the room without another word as Kalkan hurried to slip his laptop back into its case and pack the rest of his belongings into his briefcase.

Not exactly the most delicate dismissal," Hasad derided from his place on the leather couch in Recai's private office. The large room was filled with books and oversized furniture, which made even the gruff old Jew feel out of place.

"I'm not up for election Hasad; I don't have time to be nice."

Recai sat behind the large mahogany desk in a high back leather chair, looking out the window to the field of grass that should not exist. Pride in what his family had given to the city ruled his decision to bring back the loans. It was a rash, foolish decision but he needed to do something to make life in the city better. He'd let the state of his father's legacy sit long enough. He couldn't change anything. He didn't have any real power or influence. But maybe he could help someone and that might be enough. If there was no money he would fund the loans himself. He'd ignored the conditions of the people around him long enough. He had to do something. He didn't have a business mind, but he possessed the ego necessary to force his will. With Ali there to keep track of all the many ventures and divisions perhaps he could make a difference

"Nice is not something to ration."

"I don't need a lecture right now."

"Since when do I lecture? I'm an old man who's been shoveling shit around these jihadis for the last three years while you played in the desert. What could I have to say that would matter?"

"You are lecturing," Recai moaned.

"Pointing out that you are a spoiled child is not lecturing. It's a basic truth."

"I am not... I won't be baited."

Hasad settled into his seat before speaking.

"I have no worms to offer you. There are those who could substitute though, some who might be used to capture larger fist."

"I told you, I am not going along with that."

"Why?" Hasad sat up, wishing he could get through to Recai. "You liked her, call her. Go, date or court or propose or whatever you do when you want to get closer to a muslimah. Getting closer to her will get you closer to the mayor. There's no loss!"

"What if I don't want to get closer to the mayor? What if I just want to do what I can from here and not get involved? Plus Darya is not a stepping stone, I won't use her."

"And now you're being noble," Hasad snorted his disapproval.

"Hasad…"

"There are people out there dying! Women like the one you saved in the alley, women like Rebekah. We are a city without hope and we are dying. The people in the desert are dying. The country, God, everyone has turned their backs on us. You can change things. We can… *do* something!"

"What? Lecture them?" Recai petulantly retorted.

"Child!"

Recai swiveled in his chair to glare at the older man.

"You are always such pleasant company," he mumbled before leaning back and closing his eyes. Recai's body sank into the soft leather beneath him. The old man was frustrating, but he was family none the less. Bonds of grief and common purpose held the two together tightly. No matter what happened or where Recai went, Hasad would always be his friend. Rebekah's father would always have a home with him.

Hasad huffed and leaned back on the couch, sending off a cloud of dust.

"When will you let them clean this room? You spend most of your time in here; at least make it so I can breathe the air!"

Recai sighed heavily, taking in the scent of his father's cigars that still lingered, despite the years. No, he couldn't imagine having anyone clean in here. Holding close what remained of his father kept him strong, made him focus.

When he returned after his years spent in the desert, his first matter of business was to reclaim his family's home and fortune. After visiting Ali Kalkan, the Osman Corporation's Financial Advisor, it had not taken long move back into the home which had sat in escrow since his departure. Despite Ali's insistence, Recai refused to announce his return. Instead he preferred to wait until the stage was set. He staffed his home with people who hadn't known him when he'd lived there before. The city was filled with people who kept their heads down and scurried through life hoping to avoid notice. Within days of his initial arrival, the entire house had been cleaned and aired, removing the stale odor of his abandonment.

The only room he had not allowed anyone to touch was his father's office. The room was dark with an elegant chandelier high in the middle of the ceiling and brown leather furniture. Books lined the walls along with his father's most precious collections. The treasures included the sword of the Turkish sultan who had aided Hitler, a globe from the Ottoman Empire showing the spread and influence of Islam, and the official induction documents of Pasha Talat into the Grand Lodge of Free and Accepted Masons of Turkey.

Baris Osman had eclectic tastes.

Recai had played in this room as a child. He had watched his father run the business from the very chair he sat in now. The weight of his father's legacy lay heavy upon him.

"What more can I do, old man?"

As Hasad began to speak the bells rang, indicating a visitor was at the front gate. Recai sat up and used the remote in his top drawer to turn on the outdated video surveillance screen he had installed years before. At the front door stood Maryam in scrubs and *hijab* holding a newspaper up to the camera.

"Masked Protector Saves Woman from Ruin," read the headline.

Recai pressed the button to open the gate and rushed out of the room.

That night, Recai sat in his car: both hands on the steering wheel, thumbs tap-tap-tapping.

The dark had come suddenly—even the light refused to linger in this city. The streets were quiet, lending a false sense of peace. But Recai knew a man was out there with a snake wrapped around his soul. Seeing his own face in the newspaper had shocked him. He'd never imagined anyone would care what had happened in a small alley over one woman.

There had been a time when the city was safe for a woman to walk alone. He remembered skipping through the streets hand in hand with his mother, smiling and laughing. She had a way of making everyone feel at ease and could make friends with every man and woman she encountered.

"Never assume you know what's in a man's heart because of what he may look like. God shows his face in all his creations, no matter how different they may be from you."

His mother had been wise.

As the waiting began to grate on Recai's nerves and unwanted memories of his parents demanded attention, Fahri Kaya stepped out of his apartment building and headed down the street. Recai fumbled his way out of the car, his nerves frayed. He walked quickly after Fahri, following him from a safe distance.

Fahri wore his RTK uniform, a baton hung from one hip and a gun was holstered on the other. His stride was long and focused and he did not waste time looking around him—a soldier on a mission. He did not appear to be in the mood for a jovial conversation with a stranger after dark.

Swearing under his breath, Recai turned at the next block and ran, hoping to head Fahri off by approaching him from the front instead of startling him from behind. Recai jogged easily, switching automatically to the training he'd received in the Egirdir Commando.

Soon he reached the corner and peered around it, hoping to see Fahri approaching. Instead, the man had already turned and was heading away from him.

"Kahretsin!" he swore to himself, walking swiftly behind Fahri. If he surprised the officer he would have to fight him, and that was the last thing Recai wanted. He needed information from Fahri.

Recai crept forward, his steps silent upon the concrete. Fahri stepped beyond the range of the light cast by one of the few street lamps. Recai pounced. He used his advantage to overtake the officer. Pulling Fahri's arms behind his back, Recai pushed him to the ground before he could make a sound.

"Keep quiet," Recai growled, putting a knee in Fahri's back and securing a hold on the man's wrists.

"Get the fuck off of me!" Fahri yelled into the night, flailing beneath Recai's weight. Fahri struggled, not knowing that the man accosting him was only ensuring things did not become dangerous for either of them. As the RTK itself purported to believe: Sometimes, in order to keep the peace, violence was necessary.

Recai ground his knee into the struggling man's spine and at the same time he twisted Fahri's right arm clockwise and straight up, straining the flexibility of Fahri's shoulders. In this position Fahri was completely immobilized with little effort; the man's own body would cause him pain with any movement.

"Fuck you!" Fahri swore as he tried to pull himself up on his knees. Instead he only managed to push his face further into the concrete sidewalk and give Recai the chance to place his other knee strategically between his legs.

"Stop moving. I'm not going to hurt you."

Recai removed the RTK-issued baton and threw it skittering across the pavement into the night.

"What do you want?" Fahri asked, his voice strained but strong.

"I don't want to hurt you."

"Then let me go."

"I just want to ask you a question."

"Let me go, we'll get a glass of tea," Fahri sneered.

"I'm not going to let you go, but I'm not going to hurt you." Recai's voice was soft and low, forcing Fahri to strain to hear him. "I want to know how Sabiha is."

At the mention of his sister's name Fahri pitched violently, forcing Recai to rock forward so his knee cap pushed directly into his captive's spine. Fahri grunted in pain, but no one in this city would come out to help him. People barely ventured out after dark at all, let alone to investigate one of the many screams in the night.

"You leave my sister alone!"

"I just want to know if she's all right."

"Why, so you can finish what you started? Are you going to wait for her to get better and then beat her again?!"

"I didn't hurt her," Recai insisted.

"Like hell you didn't!"

"I wasn't the one who hurt her."

"Right. That's why you have me pinned to the ground in the night."

Fahri stopped struggling and laid his head down on the pavement in defeat. He knew the man above him was stronger and had the advantage. *Allah, if it pleases you, don't let me die here in the street.*

"How is Sabiha?"

Fahri gritted his teeth and remained silent. He would not give in to what he assumed was some kind of voyeuristic perversion. His sister's attack had awoken something in him. His usual disdain for anything he considered weakness was being overwhelmed by an overriding need to protect her. This, he was beginning to suspect, was his real role as the man in her life—not to marry her off, but to care for her.

This realization came at the expense of his sense of self. His life was one of which he was no longer proud. The RTK were charged with upholding the moral law of Islam, but more often than not they were the very ones breaking that code. He didn't know if his sister's attacker was RTK, but the possibility that he could be hung around his neck like a noose. It wouldn't be the first time they had been behind something like this. These thoughts ran through his mind even as he lay beneath his attacker.

"Please, is she all right? I only want to make sure she is safe," Recai pleaded.

"Why do you care?"

"I... I saw what was happening to her. I stopped it, but I didn't... I don't remember if she was still... Please, is she alright?"

Fahri took a deep breath. As afraid and confused as he felt—and as angry as that made him—he wanted to believe the man. There were so many lies in the world. So much evil.

"The nurse at the hospital said she is still a virgin, she is still pure. But even if she wasn't, she'd be safe. I . . . wouldn't have turned her out for something she had no control over."

Recai exhaled a breath he didn't mean to hold and uttered a prayer without thinking, his faith running deeper than he realized.

"Al-hamdu lillahi rabbil 'alamin."

Recai's hold on Fahri loosened and the man's shoulders burned as the tension in them relaxed. Standing, Recai dropped back under a shadow. The lamp behind him glared out every feature save his outline. They were alone, but in Elih nothing is ever really private. They spoke of things the RTK would consider treason, the stakes too high to ignore.

"You're in a lot of trouble," Fahri said, standing up and cracking his back. "You shouldn't be out here doing this."

"Doing what?" Recai whispered

"Whatever the hell it is you're doing," Fahri exclaimed in frustration.

"Your sister is safe because of me."

"And I'm in your debt. Let me repay it by telling you there are people who do not like that you are out here, people who do not like for someone else to be regarded as doing the work of Allah."

"And who exactly has been doing that work these days?"

"Are you not listening to me? Allah's work is only for the RTK here. There is no room for men like you."

"Only men like you," Recai spat.

"Only men like me.... Yes, I guess that's true. I'm one of them, even now that their cruelties have been aimed at my family; I'm still one of them."

Fahri stepped back and gazed up at the sky. There were a million stars shining above, but none of them could lead him home.

"I've not been a good man," Fahri confessed. "Or a good brother, but I'd never do this . . . at least I hope I wouldn't. I don't know anymore. I thought I was following the right path. But Sabiha never did anything to anyone, she barely spoke to anyone but me and her few friends at school. How many others have had something like this happen?"

"The RTK did this to Sabiha?" Recai ventured.

"I don't know," Fahri sighed, his own suspicions difficult to articulate. "I doubt it was a direct order, but it's hard to believe no one knew about this. The city is too tightly controlled, and there have been others."

Fahri turned to the street, instinctively checking for listeners-in.

"Who are you?" Fahri turned back, only to find the man gone. Fahri looked around but he was alone, no one there save the stars.

"I seek refuge in Allah, from the outcast Satan," he whispered.

*D*o *it,* Darya typed. She had just given final word on the order which would bring down Ali Kalkan's investigation. She'd been monitoring his emails for some time now, knowing that if anyone would notice her activities it would be the man in charge of the Osman Corporation's finances. That's what it's always about, it all comes down to who has control of the money.

The sudden interest in the Osman Corporation's accounting department had caused an unexpected halt in her uncle's incoming funds. She had always assumed her alias, "Dayar Yildirim," would allow her to conduct business without anyone knowing her gender or relation to the Yilmaz family, but interest in Osman Corp. meant interest in its Board of Directors, which could lead to someone finding out about her. Since Darya had discovered the origins of her uncle's wealth, she was confident Kalkan would do the same.

I couldn't have planned it better myself.

Darya sipped her spiced tea and once again read her half-brother's email. Who would have guessed that Ali Kalkan, the man who could bring down her entire network of finances and power, would be so exposed? All it took was one call to the bank manager in Nigeria to make sure she knew the instant he began to question the transactions she had made from the Osman's accounts into her own.

Yes, this was the beginning of something exciting. Today she would re-route all of the lines of power directly to her, reducing her uncle to nothing but a figurehead, a mouthpiece. One day, when the city was ready, she would remove him from power completely and reveal herself as the King Whisperer she really was.

Smiling, she set down her cup and reached for her *hijab*. No matter how high the temperature climbed, today she wanted to go out. There was a pair of Jimmy Choos with her name on them.

Fahri Kaya's assignment was to patrol the streets. Over the six weeks since Sabiha's attack seven more women from high-profile families were targeted. The problem was the RTK did not seem overly concerned about the welfare of the victims.

No more than two months ago, Fahri had been a proud member of the RTK. He had believed the mayor's Reformation of Turkish Kurdistan was a noble endeavor and that he was blessed to be a part of it. Plus, he enjoyed the perks that came along with being a member of the leading class. Now, however, he was not so sure. How many women had been seduced or threatened into submitting their honor? How many men had betrayed their morality for another dollar or a favor? What was the RTK reforming?

The names of the attacked women ran through his mind as he tried to find a link.

Habibeh Warda
Noor Azizi
Aasera Najafi
Baia Jaf
Fatma Serhati

Leyla Khan

Gálay Sahin

The only one who got away without dishonor was his sister: Sabiha Kaya.

Of the other victims, two committed suicide, one ran away, one had been married off to a distant family member overseas and two were missing. Fahri suspected those two were victims of honor killings, but he couldn't find any proof. His questioning of the families was met with severe reprimand from his superiors.

Up until Sabiha's attack she'd been nothing but a burden to Fahri. He had to house her because their parents were dead and it became his duty. He paid for her education because no one would want to marry her if she wasn't educated. His sister had been forced upon him, which he resented. He'd been selfish, holding her responsible for all the problems in his life.

In the end it was the Qu'ran that showed him the error of his ways. The Prophet Muhammad's, allallahu'alaihi wa sallam, said, "Only an honorable man treats women with honor and integrity. And only a mean, deceitful, and dishonest man humiliates and insults women."

When had he strayed so far?

One Saturday since her attack he had offered to take her to the bazaar in Hasankeyf. He offered to buy her some of the colorful fabric she always pined after to make new hijabs, and suggested they could have tea at one of the outdoor stands. Simple things he'd denied her in the past. The ancient fortress of Artuklu Seljucks was only a bus ride from their home but he had never taken her inside or to visit the Ulu Mosque. His new appreciation for Sabiha made him want to do more for her, to understand what it was she longed for instead of focusing on getting her out of his life.

Yet Sabiha had declined, choosing to spend her days doing the school work Aisha brought home for her and her evenings staring out the window, hoping to spot her attacker on the street.

Fahri was frustrated. He had tried to help her but she just sat in the same spot every evening, distance in her eyes. He wanted a simple life where he didn't have to take care of anyone, where he could go to work and enjoy his friends and the liberties being a member of the RTK afforded him. But now when he was invited out to one of the few bars left he couldn't help but think of his sister, alone.

Fahri turned a corner and headed into the commercial section of the city with his thoughts.. Very little activity was to be expected in this area at night. He walked quickly, looking down alleys and listening for anything out of the ordinary. His assignment was to keep the city safe from religious indiscretion, but finding The SandStorm was a higher priority for the RTK.

His visitor from the other night shook him. He didn't want to know about some vigilante in the city. He didn't want to know there were others helping him. At the same time, he hadn't reported the incident. He should have contacted his superior immediately and made a full disclosure of the conversation, but instead Fahri had gone home, leaving his duty mid-shift, to join Sabiha in her Isha prayer, the last of the day. It was the first time in five years that he had prayed outside of mandated RTK prayers.

Tonight his mind was everywhere except where it should have been—on his patrol. Instead he tried to piece together what connected the victims beyond the status of their families. Beyond his frustration at not being able to fix things, he didn't understand why he cared so much.

Fahri passed the closed, gated shops: clothiers, banks, groceries. Unlike the area of the city he lived in, where nothing was open at night, downtown was strictly for those who worked in the vicinity during the day. Even the few bars permitted to operate in Elih were closed; no one around to fill them.

117

Sudden screams crashed over him, like a typhoon upon the shore. Fahri ran, fear racing through his veins. He pushed himself to go faster.

Up ahead... Off to the right...

A woman's voice tore through the atmosphere in the abandoned city street. Her sobs beat against him with the impact of a fist as he turned the corner and found her sitting in the alley next to a trash bin, alone and unclothed.

"Who did this?" he asked, scanning the alley for the monster hunting his city.

At the sound of his voice her wails increased, and she pulled herself closer against the wall, trying to hide between the concrete and the metal of the dumpster. Fahri ran to the other end of the alley but didn't see anyone down the street. Whoever had been here was either very fast or very good at hiding.

Fahri returned to the woman, walking slowly so as not to frighten her. He put his hands out so if she looked up she would see they were empty and intentionless. Fahri crouched slightly, hoping to make himself appear smaller or less threatening. His instincts told him to hunt, to fight. Everything in him wanted to protect this woman by *doing* something. Instead he slowed his breathing and focused his eyes on what he could see of her face.

"Sister?" he asked, the word bringing visions of his own sister to mind. It was only by the grace of Allah that this hadn't happened to her.

"He... I don't know... He dragged me here and... and... and then ran off," the woman stammered.

She pulled her knees up against her chest as her shoulders shook with sobs. She wrapped her hands around her legs and pulled herself into a tight ball, as if she could create a black hole to consume everything that had happened to her.

"Sister, I am Fahri Kaya, and I am *not* going to hurt you."

I need help back here!" Maryam called out as she stepped into the next triage room to find her patient, Bey Qureshi, a local handyman, holding a bloody rag over his hand. She dropped the chart she'd been carrying onto a table and rushed to his side.

"What did you do?"

She pulled the rag off of his hand and inspected the almost severed digit. Quickly she reached for gauze from the drawer next to the bed, wrapped the wound tightly, and held his hand up over her head.

"I'm not feeling right," the man replied as his flesh grew pale and clammy.

"I need help!" She held his hand tightly, keeping the pressure on the wound. "Bey Qureshi, can you tell me who brought you in? Is someone here with you?"

"I drove here my..." the man slurred, slumping back against the hospital bed.

"Come on!" she called.

Doctor Basara opened the door.

"What are you going on about in here?"

"He's nearly cut off his left index finger and has been bleeding for a while. He passed out just now and seems to be—"

Maryam was cut off mid-sentence by the young doctor's bark.

"Ai'sha!" he called to the nurse rushing in behind him, always ready to fall into step behind Doctor Basara. Her *hijab* was loose and a wisp of chocolate-brown hair hung in her face. She met Maryam's eyes and mouthed *sorry* with a shrug, a little too easily.

Doctor Basara strode into the room and took the injured man's arm from where Maryam held it elevated. He was one of

119

the younger residents at Dunya Hastanesi, and he resented Maryam's position among the staff. He saw her as only a nurse, and yet she managed to command more respect than he did.

"Did you get his vitals?"

"I called for help as soon as I saw the extent of his injury."

"So you didn't get his vitals. You have done nothing that would help me evaluate his condition."

"The chart's on the table," Maryam stated before walking out of the room and heading toward the nurse's station to wash her hands. Although she sent up a silent prayer that Bey Qureshi didn't lose his finger completely, she was glad to be away from Basara.

"Dorri, I'm taking my break," she said to the charge nurse.

"Basara?" the woman asked without pause in the click-click-click of her fingers against the computer's keyboard.

"Who else?"

"I'll be glad when he marries Fatma and they both go away," another of the nurses chimed in with a wicked twinkle in her eye.

"You think?"

Dorri stopped typing, eager for new gossip.

"Her hijab has been looser."

"I smelled bleach on her the other day; I think she's been dying her hair *blonde*."

"He does always ask for her help if she's on staff."

"He just likes a sycophant; he's not interested in her," Maryam contributed.

"Sisters, gossip is a sin," a short, heavy set muslimah scolded, stopping their chatter. The nurses bowed their heads to ask Allah's forgiveness for their loose tongues.

Maryam smiled and stepped away, not in the mood for the gossip or the lesson. She walked outside into the thick heat of the city. She leaned against the wall and closed her eyes, wishing she was basking in the sun on the beach near her childhood home, or that an oasis breeze was wafting over her. Her shift was almost over and she had to shower and change before returning to

Osman Estates. She wasn't sure yet what she had gotten herself into by agreeing to meet with Hasad and Recai, but she knew there was no time for second-guessing; something in the city had to change and if anyone could do it, it was Recai.

Once a thing is set into motion, it must be seen through.

"Maryam!" Dorri's voice broke through Maryam's introspection. "Maryam, we need you!"

The frantic sound of Dorri's voice sent a wave of panic down her spine. Her stomach knotted up as she began to run. She knew what that voice meant.

Not another one...

ahri had called in the attack, but no one ever came to investigate. None of the RTK patrol cars arrived to take the poor woman to the hospital, and soon the central office told him to stop calling. This attack was not going to be investigated.

After countless attempts to reason with the woman, explaining that he would not hurt her, Fahri covered her with his uniform jacket and forcibly picked her up, enduring her flailing arms and scratching nails. He carried her the entire two miles to the hospital. Eventually she gave up her fight and wept against his neck.

Stepping into the hospital was like returning to a waking nightmare. This was the same waiting room where he had sat while his sister was examined; the same florescent lights blinded his eyes as he called out for someone to help him with his burden. But he would have walked another two miles before abandoning this woman in the street. If The SandStorm hadn't helped Sabiha she'd have been raped or worse. Now he had a turn to pay his due.

As soon as they saw him, the nurses swarmed and ushered him into a small room away from the main treatment rooms. A heavyset *muslimah* with a puckered mouth was the first to speak.

"Did you do this?" she accused as soon as the woman was out of his arms.

The other nurses ignored his scratched face and bustled about the room, getting an IV into the girl's arm and checking her vitals.

"No!" Fahri exclaimed, guilt flooding his features because he knew it wasn't unreasonable to think an RTK officer had done such a thing. "I was patrolling downtown and I found her. She was screaming. I carried her here."

The woman took a moment to evaluate his words and manner before further puckering her mouth, nodding, and walking out.

Fahri moved awkwardly out from under the remaining nurses' feet. They went about their business as the violated woman cried softly. Finally, out of options of places to stand, he sat in one of a pair of stiff plastic chairs pushed against the wall and studied the tile on the floor. His presence in the room with the injured woman in this state of undress was improper, but he couldn't leave her. He wouldn't leave her alone. She may be a stranger, but until her family arrived he was all she had.

Soon the heavyset woman and another nurse rushed in.

"Assalaamu alum, Sister," the new nurse said, standing at the end of the bed. Fahri risked a look up and noticed that the other nurses were leaving the three of them alone. When the crying victim did not speak, the only sound she was capable of making a soft whimpering, the nurse turned her attention to Fahri.

"Assalaamu alum."

"Walaikum as salaam," he replied, his eyes on the foot of the bed of the crying woman.

"My name is Maryam Al-Gamdi," she began. "I'm going to need to examine this woman. The more you can tell me about what happened the easier it's going to be for me to help her."

Fahri nodded, bringing his eyes to Maryam's.

"What is your name?" she asked.

"Fahri Kaya, lieutenant in the RTK, Third Division, Lion Team."

"Fahri?"

"Yes," he confirmed, confusion knitting his brow together as she studied him.

"Do you know this woman?"

"No, I found her while I was on patrol."

"What is her name?" Maryam continued, keeping all inflection and assumption out of her voice.

"I don't know. She . . . she was already like this when I found her."

"Has she spoken to you at all?"

"No, she screamed a lot and scratched me."

Fahri turned his face so Maryam could see where the woman had lashed out when he'd picked her up to take her to the hospital.

"She hasn't said anything about who she is or what happened," he continued.

"Lieutenant Kaya, did you hurt this woman?" Maryam tilted her head to the side as she asked the question, an expectant look on her face.

"Allahu Akbar, no!"

Fahri stood up to pace, but finding the room too small, he sat down again, his legs bouncing in their need for movement.

"I didn't think so."

Maryam sat down next to him before whispering, barely loud enough for him to hear: "I believe we have a mutual friend. The man who rescued your sister—you spoke to him, did you not?"

Pouring over the lines of an accounts-payable audit trail report, Ali Kalkan sipped his tea. He had printed everything out; thousands of pages sat in piles around him. Osman Enterprises was supposed to be a "paperless" corporation, but Ali preferred doing things the old fashioned way. He could write in the margins and mark pages to revisit and investigate further.

Ali was making progress. Seven of the thirteen unaccounted-for ledger entries could be tracked back to foreign accounts: one in the United States, three in Iraq, two in Britain, and one in Pakistan. The accounts were set up on different days in different names, but they all siphoned the same percentage off of the interest-bearing annuity.

Four billion dollars had been drawn off of the main accounts through complex channels. Small amounts transferred between internal accounts, replenishing balances, offsetting expenses. All with justified account details. But each time it happened, the amount deposited was slightly less than the amount transferred. Unremarkable discrepancies occurring over the past four years throughout all of the company's accounts: checking, operational, investment, savings.

Eventually he had found it. Each transfer included an automatic internal wire to an account in Nigeria. When Ali compared the wire history to the transaction detail, he found the pattern. Now all he had to do was find who owned the foreign account.

Ali enjoyed the hunt, the cat-and-mouse of forensic accounting Now that he was making headway his own arrogance fueled him on. Two plus two equaled four, except when it didn't. The possible reasons for the shortfall were infinite, and tracking down the missing data invigorated Ali in a way he hadn't felt in years.

Ali turned back to his computer. An alert he had placed on the account for any new wire transfers had been sent to his email. He allowed the transfer to go through, but delayed it, having the bank contact the Nigerian asset manager receiving the funds. Sifting through the raw data supplied by the bank, each line adding color and dimension to the overall picture, Ali's eyes strained.

The answer was here. He went through it again and again until hidden within lines of code he found the detail he had been looking for: an automatic router to a domestic account. Now he had the numbers he needed to find who had been stealing from the Osmans.

The phone in his pocket vibrated and then rang with the tone of an old fashioned phone.

"Hello?"

"Bey Kalkan"? The voice on the other end of the phone inquired.

"Yes, who is this?" Ali replied.

"This is Maryam Al-Gamdi. I am a nurse at Dunya Hastanesi."

"How can I help you Beyan Al-Gamdi?" Ali asked, nervousness gripping his spine.

"I'm afraid your daughter Aysel, has been in an accident, and we need you to come down to the hospital." Ali heard this stranger say.

He stood up. The rolling chair he had been sitting in slid back into the wall behind him.

"Is she alright? May I speak with her?"

"Yes, she is fine. She's having some tests done now and may have some broken ribs, but she will recover with no problems. What she really needs now is for someone to come be with her."

"Of course, my wife will be there as soon as I call her," Ali agreed, feeling some relief.

"Bey Kalkan, I'm afraid that in this case we need you to come down and sign her out," the voice belonging to the nurse calmly stated.

"Why?"

There were few things his wife couldn't do in his stead. Ali's brow beaded with sweat despite the powerful air conditioner that cooled his home. What could have happened that would require him to go down personally?

"If it's possible, it would be best for you to come to the hospital, and I will explain everything when you get here. Your daughter will be fine, but she needs her family with her."

"But my wife cannot be the one to bring her home?" Ali insisted, refusing to give in to what he knew.

"No."

'So a male family member needs to come down and sign her paperwork, is that what you are telling me?" Ali insisted.

"In this case, yes, we need you to come down to the hospital."

"What kind of accident did you say she was in?"

"She wasn't badly injured…" the nurse's voice faltered in Ali's ear.

"Beyan, I'm sorry for being rude, but I asked you a question. I expect you to answer."

Ali paced, moving around his room without an intended destination. Instinct told him to rush out of the house and pull his daughter into his arms. But something held him back; something about the nurse's tone frightened him to his core.

"Your daughter was attacked," was her curt reply.

Ali stilled. The room froze around him as fear curled around his heart.

"Was she… Beyan, can you tell me what kind of attack it was?"

"The kind she'll recover from. But we need you to come down to the hospital."

"Is her . . . ? Was she . . . ? What I mean to ask is… is her honor intact?" Ali forced himself to ask.

"Your daughter has done nothing wrong."

"Was she raped?" he demanded, tired of running around in circles with the woman on the phone.

"Bey, you should just come down to the hospital."

"Was she raped?!"

"Yes."

The phone line was silent, but Ali heard the tension on the other end. He loved his daughter, more than words could express. But he held the responsibility to protect himself, his family, and his other daughters from this shame. With a tear of regret in his eye Ali hung up the phone.

*T*he wave broke around his legs as he stared up at the stars. The constellations were familiar but in the wrong places in the sky, as if they had all been pulled along as the sun set. It was a night with no moon, but the stars shone brightly, reflecting off of the tide, whispering their secrets to those who would listen.

Recai dove into the next wave, allowing the cool water to rush over his body.

Coming up for air he found himself farther out than he expected, surrounded by nothing but water. The coastline had faded into the distance, and it was just Recai and the expansive nothingness. The water rippled around him, the starlight twinkling above.

Instead of panic, Recai felt only a deep and complete sense of peace. He allowed his body to float up, bobbing atop the salty water. With his legs relaxed, dipping down into the black beneath him, he spread his arms and welcomed the freedom of isolation.

"Recai"

The voice vibrated in the water around him. He lifted his head and pulled his body beneath him so he could tread water and look around. There was no movement in the silent sea apart from the ripples created by his slowly kicking legs.

"Hello?" the night absorbed the sound of his voice.

Disoriented, Recai dove under, hoping for the clean refreshing water to reorganize his thoughts.

"Recai..."

The voice came again as soon as his head dipped under the water, but was gone as he burst to the surface, scanning the horizon and again finding nothing.

He filled his lungs and dove down, forcefully pushing himself as deep as he could go.

"Recai, have you forgotten me?"

A sweet familiar voice filled his mind.

"Where are you?" He screamed into the water, using what little air he had left. Bubbles exploded into the black water drifting upward.

"I am with you, always. Have you forgotten your promise so soon?"

"Rebekah?"

Recai stopped his frantic search beneath the surface, out of air and finally out of time.

It was late by the time Maryam left the hospital. Her old car got her home safely as always, and she parked in the lot two blocks from her building. The night had been difficult and exhausting.

Hospital politics and her own good sense were so often in conflict she wondered how she managed to work there at all.

Because if I didn't, who would have made sure the Kalkan girl had somewhere to sleep tonight? If I wasn't there, where would she have gone?

Maryam had a friend who attended the only Greek Orthodox Church in town. It was small and not well attended, but the church was tolerated by the RTK, an essential political move on the part of the Mayor to keep anyone from looking too closely at the small city. When a woman was left unclaimed by her family after being dishonored her options were slim, but if she was lucky and Maryam was on duty, some would receive refuge at the church.

Aysel Kalkan had left the hospital without ever being officially admitted, without any record of what she had endured, and without her father ever coming to retrieve her. She left and would be safe, that much the nurses at Dunya Hastanesi could provide. The rest was up to her.

Stepping out of her car, Maryam tightened her *hijab*, glad she had brought clothes to change into so she didn't have to walk so late at night in her scrubs. In the hospital it didn't bother her to wear pants of such thin fabric; it was a part of her job, a uniform like any other. But on the streets, she much preferred the familiarity and comfort of her *abaya*.

Maryam was lost in thought as she walked down the dark street that led her home. She didn't see Abdullah's figure until he stepped out into the glow of the street lamp, a thin, hand-rolled cigarette in his hand.

"Abdullah!" she cried, unsettled by her grocer's sudden appearance. Something within her recoiled from him, even though he was a familiar and friendly face.

"Maryam, you're home late." His intonation was flat.

"The hours of a nurse," she shrugged and resumed walking toward home.

"You shouldn't be out so late alone."

"I'm fine, thank you for worrying about me." Maryam gave a strained smile, a nagging worry in the back of her mind. "Was the store open late tonight?"

Abdullah fell into step next to her, his hair bobbing around his ears as he walked, his smile full and bright. The return of the friendly Abdullah she knew relaxed her and she smiled in return.

"No, the store closed as usual. I had been hoping you would stop in, and when you didn't I waited."

"Abdullah, that's kind but unnecessary."

"I told you the other day I worry about you living alone in the city."

"Please, don't worry. I am used to it now. I like living alone."

Abdullah laughed with a full throaty voice.

"No woman likes living alone!"

"Well it suits me fine for now."

Maryam's smile was strained once again. The door to her building was just one more block, but it looked like Abdullah had no intention of leaving her side.

"Only because you are not married. If you were married you would have a family and children to nurse, no need for hospitals and late nights alone."

Silence was her only response. Abdullah's crush on her had worked to her advantage so far, but had she encouraged him too much? Had she tempted him in some way she hadn't intended? Again she felt thankful for changing out of her scrubs and she pulled her hands up into the sleeves of her abaya, hiding as much of herself from Abdullah's gaze as possible.

"Maryam, would you like to be married?"

"Someday, perhaps, but for now I am enjoying my work."

She increased her pace, hoping someone would be out smoking in front of her building as the men who lived on the other floors sometimes did.

"I think you enjoy your work because you don't have anything else. Perhaps if you had a child and a husband you'd be fulfilled instead of trying to find happiness through work."

"Abdullah, it's late. I think you should go home."

"Not until I know you are safe."

"I am safe. I walk home every day alone; tonight is no different."

"There have been more attacks."

His voice was low and had lost some of its playfulness.

"I work in the Emergency Department. I know all about the dangers of the city, and still I am fine to walk alone."

Maryam lifted her head higher and drew on strength she didn't quite have as she approached her door. It was abandoned to the night, no one outside at this hour.

Abdullah stopped next to the door, situating himself so Maryam would need to reach past him to put her key in the lock. Her building was only four stories high, with the grocery on the ground floor, the second floor for women tenants only, and the two top floors for men. There was no doorman, only a maintenance man who lived on the third floor and didn't fix anything.

"You should marry," Abdullah blurted.

"Someday, when the time is right."

"You should marry me."

"Abdullah!"

"Someday, when the time is right," he smiled broadly.

Abdullah's dark skin contrasted sharply against his white teeth, making him look like a smile without a body. A beat passed before he stepped away from her with a glint in his eye. Maryam unlocked her door and stepped inside, unable to breathe again until she heard the click of the deadbolt snap into place.

Imam Al-Bashir kneeled alone in the mosque facing the quibla for the early-morning prayer. He kept his focus in the direction of Mecca and waited for others to arrive. Every day, five times a day, he did this. Perhaps this would be one of those times when a straggler or sinner would make their way here. If not, he would prostrate before Allah and vow to minister to those who needed him.

The call for prayer, no longer performed by a *muezzin* but instead a recorded voice, echoed out over the wealthy neighborhood:

Allaahu Akbar
Allaahu Akbar
Allaahu Akbar
Allaahu Akbar

Ash'hadu an laa ilaaha illallaah
Ash'hadu an laa ilaaha illallaah
Ash'hadu anna Muhammadan-rasulullaah
Ash'hadu anna Muhammadan-rasulullaah

Haya 'alas-salaah
Haya 'alas-salaah
Haya 'alal falaah
Haya 'alal falaah

Allaahu Akbar
Allaahu Akbar

The sound echoed in the emptiness within the grand prayer hall.

With a sigh, Al-Bashir stood and began the movements that corresponded with his prayer. The ritual was so embedded in his body the individual steps were unimportant; the sequence cleansed his mind and soul.

Standing, he raised his hands to heaven in reverence and then folded them one over the other upon his breast, opening his heart to the love of Allah. Al-Bashir enjoyed the ritual of prayer. As he bowed, he placed his hands softly upon his knees. He felt the warmth of Allah spread over him. In his mind he recited passages from the Qu'ran, centering and focusing his mind on the peace promised to the faithful. Finally he lowered himself to the ground in sajdah, laying his body prostrate on the prayer rug in complete submission. With deep breaths he released his vanity and selfish desires, making room within his heart for the love and wisdom of Allah to guide him.

After performing the rak'ah four times Al-Bashir sat, eyes closed. He easily pulled prayers from his mind, having begun memorizing the Holy Book, reciting it rote while sitting at the feet of his father, before he could read or write.

There is no God but Allah, and He shall be glorified most high.

Softly, the faithful man opened his eyes to the barren room. Sadness entered his heart. "Peace on you and the mercy of Allah," he whispered to all of the souls who had forgotten the importance of worship. Mayor Yilmaz and his RTK had forced the external trappings of religion down the people's throats. The compulsory acts were driving people away from the mosque instead of into the house of Allah. Each day, men and women were forced to conduct themselves in ways conscripted from the secular world instead of finding their way to embracing Islam.

The Ummah is dying from within. Al-Bashir's fears for his people grew every day. Each day he saw zina, vanity and sin.

The pillars of his religion were falling around him, leaving the city in ruins. The few who proclaimed true faith fell into two categories, the pseudo-Muslims who do not practice the tenants of their religion but make quite a big show of it in public, and the jihadists. Perhaps in the city's other mosques this wasn't the case, but here, in Aydinkonak, the mosque was empty.

What am I to do? Al-Bashir prayed: *There is no power and no strength save in Allah...*

Recai awoke with a start, coughing and sputtering as if he had water in his lungs.

Her name was on his lips as he kicked off the covers and pulled on a pair of jeans. He'd passed through unconsciousness and woke to the nightmare of having been left behind. Unlike the Queen of Sheba, it seemed he did have nine lives.

How many more must I suffer before I am released from this earth?

He stumbled around in the darkness for a moment, disoriented within his own room. He had fallen asleep unexpectedly after dinner, unable to focus any longer on business or Hasad's increasingly annoying lectures. The night was black, and when he looked out his window he could find no moon.

A night with no moon... Rebekah...

Recai pulled on a shirt and stuffed his feet into the shoes lying on the floor before grabbing his keys and heading out into the darkness.

He pulled his Marussia B2 out of the estate's large garage and toward the streets of the city without turning on the headlights or switching on the radio—he preferred the silence of the abandoned neighborhoods. With his windows down the heat rushed through the car, bringing with it the scent of the desert. Overhead a flash of lightning lit the sky, exposing the orange hue that preceded a sandstorm.

Above, the stars were being snuffed out one by one before him as the night sky became opaque and thick. The acrid scent of burning sand filled the air and rode on the wind, warning all in its path of looming destruction.

The idea of driving into the kum firtinasi entertained Recai as memories of the deaths he should have had swarmed around him. How many times must a man be expected to survive? How many deaths must he witness and be helpless to stop before he can succumb?

Except Sabiha. Sabiha is alive!

Recai sped down the side streets without direction as his mind focused on other, more upsetting thoughts. He lived in the shadow of the parents he had lost, hiding in a past he'd rather forget. He had spent his life wandering, purposeless, never accomplishing anything because of his own self doubt.

Except Sabiha.

Soon the city shrank behind him, the light of civilization reaching up to the heavens and reflecting back the orange glow of the storm. Before him there was no light and nothing but the sand.

Since his time living with the Kurdish nomads after Rebekah's death, Recai had come to think of the desert as a refuge, a place outside of the demands of real life. He missed the simplicity and ease of disappearing into the sea of sand. His car roared, speeding toward the end of the world, prepared to drive off the edge and into the abyss.

The wind picked up, whipping the sand it carried into a cyclone, feeding on its own power and ferocity. Sand beat against the car. Tiny particles ate into the paint and enamel, stripping away everything but speed and power as Recai raced further into nothing.

Soon the storm was too severe, and Recai couldn't see the road ahead. Sand blew into the car through the open window and infiltrated the air vents, causing grit to fill his mouth with each breath. Stopping the car, he pushed the door open and ran toward the building chaos.

"I'm here!" he called to the heavens. "I'm here and there's nothing to stop you this time. Take me! Free me! I'm no good here! I can't do anything! I don't know what you want of me, but I can't do it. Allah, I seek refuge from you!"

The wind howled in response as electricity crackled and sparked in the sky.

With his arms spread out above him Recai closed his eyes. The storm surrounded him and beat against his body. His thin shirt offered little protection and his skin stung. But he stood, braving the elements, wishing to disappear into the ferocity of the storm, to become one with it, to leave himself behind.

"Recai..."

The voice from his dream called to him, and the wind rushed past, making it impossible to breathe. The oxygen pushed out from the eye of the storm, creating an emptiness around him. Only sand and heat filled Recai's lungs as he struggled for breath, his eyes watering as the reality of the danger around him solidified.

"I am with you, always."

Recai fell to the ground as he struggled for breath. The voice that haunted him whispered as his eyes streamed tears and the sand built up around him. So much sand swam in the sky it was as if the earth itself were being ground to powder.

A crack rang out, sounding like the gates of Jahannam had broken open, and the devils themselves were rushing toward him, surrounding Recai with their hellfire. Lightning blazed in the sky and the electricity of the atmosphere intensified until it coalesced into one final thunderbolt, which blazed with the hottest fire and trailed pillars of black smoke. Recai called out to the angel Malik to release him as a thunderbolt rocked through the storm and struck true.

PART 4

"THINGS ARE NOT WHAT THEY APPEAR TO BE: NOR ARE THEY OTHERWISE."

Surangama Sutra

Darya slammed the phone down after reaching her uncle's voicemail for the seventh time.

Two hours!

She had waited for two hours for him to come meet her. He had requested this meeting; he had insisted they discuss the current "structure" face-to-face. All along she worked in the background, twisting and manipulating the leaders of the RTK with various pressure points. Some had weaknesses to exploit, while others had ambitions of their own. The last two years had been dedicated to finding and using every leverage she had.

The money was the final stage. She had been slowly siphoning off the investments into an account in the name of her pseudonym, Dayar Yildirim. There was a second set of documents, a second set of accounts, a second life, all in the name her uncle gave her to hide his need for a woman to run things for him.

Uncle Mahmet was weak, just like the rest of them. Sex, power, greed, shame—with men it was always something. The trick was to find the soft underbelly and strike with precision.

The longer she waited the more agitated she became, anticipating his arrival. She busied herself with email and other tasks, but checking on the various accounts and investments she had only occupied so much time. All of the work she had to do required a kind of dedicated focus she didn't currently possess. She itched to leave her small downtown office and not be here when he finally arrived. That's what she would have done to anyone else who had the audacity to keep her waiting, but this altercation was overdue. It was time for her to receive some respect and compensation for the work she did. It was time for the power of Elih to know that Dayar *is* Darya.

Perhaps she would call Recai. His green eyes hadn't left her mind since she'd first met him at her uncle's party. He was different from the others she knew in Elih. They were all either philanderers parading as pious men, or bound to the outdated concepts of sexuality and modesty her religion dictated. The proper and expected behavior was to wait: wait for Recai to call, wait for him to inquire about her to her uncle or his friends. He would never contact her directly. Or perhaps he would. Recai was a man even death couldn't contain, so perhaps he wasn't interested in the rules of society. But then, why hadn't she heard from him?

A caged animal desperate for release, she prowled her office restlessly. She yearned to claw and rip at the world that kept her confined. This is why she'd never been a good daughter, or a good Muslim, and why she'd never be a good wife. Dreams of escape occupied her every thought. It was wrong, but she couldn't fight her nature.

The evening sun filtered through the blinds that blocked passersby from seeing into the back room of her office. Even here she was hidden. The front room was a façade; no one worked there or staffed the desk elegantly labeled "Reception." Darya spent most of her days alone, though occasionally she would meet with an investor or a client.

In the corner of her office stood an ornate screen that hid a small desk behind it. She would sit there during meetings, and act as Dayar's secretary, adding another layer to her humiliation and isolation. She couldn't speak with them as herself when the mere presence of a woman in business meetings was so offensive she had to hide herself. At first clients had insisted on speaking with Bey Yildirim in person, but soon they came to accept Darya as his emissary. Millions of dollars passed through her hands as easily as sand sifted though the fingers of a child, and still, her face could not be seen.

Located in the high-priced Safak district, the small space was situated on the ground floor of one of the more elegant buildings in the city. Everyone who passed by either to shop in the high-end stores or dine at one of the many international restaurants saw the sign on her door: Dayar Yildirim, Investment Manager. Every day she entered through that same door and every day her resentment and anger grew.

From behind the screen she negotiated the deals and intimidated the men who now answered to her above their families, above Allah. She held the keys to the kingdom. Today her uncle was coming to try and snatch them back.

Darya glared at the phone, more determined than ever. She held her head high and grabbed her hijab from where it was draped over a guest chair. Wrapping her hair and face in the thin black veil, she swore to herself she would never wait for any man again.

H ere!" Hasad cried when he spotted Recai's half-buried Marussia.

His arthritic finger pointed to the left from the passenger seat, reaching in front of Maryam's face, causing her to flinch back in surprise. The vehicle they rode in was large, but he was still close enough for the motion to temporarily block her view. Swerving, Maryam steered the Hummer they had requisitioned from Recai's garage in the direction Hasad pointed. Sand spun under the wheels for a moment before they found traction and sped forward.

The Marussia B2 looked more like a cartoon than a car to Hasad. It was covered in sand. The storm had moved an entire dune from its original place to directly on top of the vehicle. The back end was buried but the front and driver's side protruded from the edge of the dune's incline.

Premature relief flooded through Maryam. *If his car is here, perhaps he is as well.*

Living in Recai's house was uncomfortable for the old man, who was accustomed to making his own way. The house sat eerily still without Recai's presence, making Hasad even more uncomfortable. Hasad found himself spending the time in the senior Osman's office sorting through newspapers, looking for a chink in the armor of the RTK. But his worry mounted when he realized just how long Recai had been gone.

Finally, he had called Maryam, too early to yet be considered morning, but it was as late as he could stand to wait. The television had no reports of anyone notable having been injured, and he didn't dare call hospitals and risk alerting anyone of Recai's disappearance. The nurse who placed so much faith in them—for no reason Hasad could conceive—proved to be the only person he trusted.

Hasad's mind wandered to his unlikely partner in the driver's seat of the Hummer. She was a Muslim and he a Jew, and yet he felt protective of her and impressed by her open heart. She had treated him as an equal despite his age and religion. She had helped Recai and Sabiha despite the risk because it was the right thing to do. Too many people take the easy path. If Maryam could see the goodness in people and work to make things better it really didn't matter by what name she called her God.

"The boy is stupid. There's no reason to doubt it. Been trying to kill himself since the first time I met him."

Hasad had been ranting for hours, his concern and annoyance with Recai growing in direct proportion to the amount of time the man was missing.

"He's not stupid, he's… impetuous," Maryam defended Recai.

"Stupid."

"He's just prone to the dramatic."

Hasad stepped down from the passenger's side once Maryam stopped the car and stormed toward the sand-filled vehicle. Her heart stopped in her chest for a beat as she took in the sheer magnitude of the dune before them. She didn't spend much time in the desert. Having grown up by the water, the sight of so much sand without a sea made her feel exposed and panicky. She worried that at any moment she might disappear into the expanse around her and no one would ever know.

"Besides, his theatrics sometimes work to his benefit," she called after Hasad.

"Stupid. Look at this, the windows are down! Stupid!"

Hasad thrust his hands into the driver's window and began searching in the dry sand. It drifted out the window as he pushed his arm deeper within. Scooping out armfuls of sand, Hasad let it filter to the ground at his feet before reaching in further. Its dry grains stuck to his wrinkled hands and sucked the moisture from his skin. His heart clenched with each handful that passed through his fingers.

Maryam watched the old man's frantic search, unsure how to help. If Recai had come out here alone during a kum firtinasi, the chances he'd survived weren't strong. But she believed in him. His arrogant, indulgent and dramatic ways aside, she believed Recai was a good man, and after what she had seen at the hospital over the past few weeks she questioned how many good men there were left in Elih. Rapes were common in the city, but the past few weeks it seemed there was another every day. It was all she could do to keep her faith intact.

Wherever Recai was, he had to be alive; her faith in humanity depended on it.

"Well, there doesn't seem to be a body behind the wheel anyway," Hasad snorted, pulling his torso out of the window and looking up at the sky. Desperation filled his eyes with tears.

Where could he be?

"He's fine," Maryam insisted automatically for the seventy-thousandth time.

"He knows how to survive in the desert; he knows how to get away from the winds."

"If he wants to…"

Hasad's tone was desperate; he feared he'd lost the only person who understood his pain—his son by death and guilt.

The desert muffled all sound, an arid void within which it was easy to forget who you were or where you were going. Maryam looked around, imagining how easy it would be to disappear here, to lose herself into the nothingness surrounding her. She was thankful for the colorful hijab she had donned this morning; the contrast against the sand might make her body easier to find.

"He's fine," she said again, more to herself than Hasad.

With a grunt and a pass of the hand over his face, Hasad headed toward the edge of the dune. He had spent the better part of the last twenty years out here in the desert. He understood how to avoid an avalanche and navigate the drifts. His body moved to the shifting rhythm of the sand.

"You Muslims aren't supposed to try to kill yourselves are you?" Hasad's tone was mocking, but waves of grief emanated from him.. "Why does this idiot-boy insist on doing every stupid thing he can think of?"

Maryam followed Hasad without responding, imitating the man's steps as she moved across the sand. Her own concern ate at her from within. Had she been wrong to place so much faith in a man she didn't know? Had she been wrong to dream of change?

Plodding forward, the two rounded the curve of the dune. The expanse before them was massive and empty. Sand flowed before them in all directions. They were at the center of the earth. Everything that had ever existed coalesced here. Time seemed to stand still in the desert.

After twenty minutes of hiking through the shifting terrain, Hasad stopped and slumped down to the ground, setting his weight in the sand. His back curved forward and for a moment Maryam stood in front of him and could see the old man Hasad really was. Years of pain and grief shone in his eyes as he peered out into the distance, searching for everything he'd lost.

"Effendi…"

"Stop calling me that," he grunted without looking up at her. He shouldn't have called her. She was another attachment, another emotional investment he could not afford. Perhaps he was the reason for all this pain, perhaps simply by knowing her he would predetermine her death.

"No."

"Why do none of you listen to me? I'm not Turkish and I'm not Muslim and I'm not someone you should look up to! Don't call me that."

"You are Effendi to me," Maryam stated as she curled her legs beneath her and sat next to him.

"We're never going to find him like this."

"He's survived out here before."

"Barely."

They sat in silence as the sun rose higher in the sky, assaulting the desert with its unforgiving heat.

Ali Kalkan sat at his desk, staring at a picture of his three daughters. Aysel had been his youngest, the sweetest of his girls. He had called her 'Tatim' and held her on his lap when she was young, reading her stories about the Prophet's daughter Fatimah and the Israelite Asiyah. And now she was gone.

Aysel's death was as certain to Ali as was the fact that his office door was closed and that the street lights would come on at sunset. He had raised her to be honorable, to have pride in herself. Any woman of moral character would make the right decision after such disgrace. While mourning, he was also proud of her. That she may not have taken her own life never occurred to him.

The timing between her attack and his investigation into the missing funds was not lost on him. Nor was the veiled threat he'd received from the bank manager in Nigeria when he'd called. His inquiries into the identity of the account owner were not received well, and somehow the man had known his daughter's name.

He stared at the picture. Continuing his investigation into the money missing from the Osman accounts would put them all at risk, but what kind of man would he be if he didn't? There was no easy answer and his commitment to his family was stronger than his allegiance to the Osmans, no matter how much he owed them.

Ali sighed and opened a drawer on the left side of his desk. He took out the heavy weight monogrammed paper his wife had bought him when he'd been promoted to Head Accountant and wrote one name. The name that would lead Recai to his answers. The name that would haunt him as long as he had daughters living in Elih.

Dayar Yildirim

It was midmorning on the day *after* Darya's scheduled meeting with her uncle and she still had not heard from him. The confidence she'd felt when she'd walked out of her office the evening prior waned as she sat before her laptop at the small desk she used at home. Analyzing the numbers from last week's investments allowed her mind to focus on the task before her and avoid her emotions, which vacillated between outright terror at his silence to exuberance at the upcoming confrontation.

She stood and stretched, enjoying her tired muscles after the women-only yoga class she'd attended that morning. It was one of her rare public activities. Generally, Darya did not get along with women. *Because they are weak.*

Grabbing her cooling cup of coffee, she opened the large doors leading out to the patio. The sand from the kum firtinasi had settled, burying those unfortunate enough to live at the bottom of the world. Here, in her penthouse, Darya could breathe and enjoy the sprawling city beneath her. In the distance, a single lightning bolt lit up the sky over the desert.

Residual electricity sparked in the air.

Change comes unexpectedly in times of high pressure.

ehydration motivated Maryam. It was almost noon and they had been sitting watching the dunes for hours. No movement, other than the occasional bird-of-prey overhead. As they sat, Hasad aged and Maryam worried.

"Effendi, let's go. We can come back with supplies and search."

"No."

"Sitting here isn't going to help him or help us find him. We can't walk farther out into that," Maryam said gesturing toward the expansive desert.

A crack of thunder and single bolt of lightning burst from the sky, landing within feet of where they sat. Maryam jumped back with a scream, moving her hand to her heart.

With a steadying breath, Maryam tried to reassure herself. *Just another storm.* The flash of lightning had been close and the atmosphere tasted burnt in her mouth.

"An electrical storm?" she asked.

"No," Hasad stood and surveyed the sky. "There are no clouds."

He stepped toward where the air had sparked.

"Those don't happen often here, and never with only one thunderbolt. There should be more flashing in the sky. But now it's quiet again . . ." his voice trailed off as his eyes unfocused, taking in the vast emptiness.

Maryam's nerves were heightened. Her fear for Recai combined with the freak lightning and threatened to push her into a panic.

"Let's go," she said with a shaking voice.

"No."

"What if it happens again?"

Maryam's tone was nervous, pleading. She didn't like being out here in the open; the stillness of the air made her anxious.

Hasad took a step forward, and then another. He wandered out farther, not hearing Maryam's pleas for him to come back with her. He ventured out toward the gentle slope of a small dune. A song in the sizzling air called him forward, beckoning him to the place where the sand was singed from the lightning's contact.

"Hasad!" Maryam called, chasing after him clumsily on legs unaccustomed to walking on a moving landscape. "Where are you going? We have to go back!"

Wind gusted over them, chilling their skin as their sweat evaporated. Then the gust ended as suddenly as it had begun, but the sand it swept up still moved in the air around them. Each particle drifted sideways against gravity, circling the two unlikely allies. When Maryam reached Hasad he pulled her to him protectively.

The air quivered as the sand hung suspended.

Standing together, surrounded by the impossible reality of magic, the two held one another tightly. The young woman allowed herself to be sheltered from the djinn dance around them, fearing that this may be the moment she submitted to death.

Above them the sky cracked open with a deafening boom. The reverberation of the sound hit them like a wave, taking the dancing sand with it as it spread over the desert. Lightning flashed again, blinding them with its light. Their skin sizzled with the heat.

Maryam screamed and pulled away from Hasad's embrace. Instinct told her to flee the danger around her.

Lightning struck the ground nearby, corralling her and forcing her back into Hasad's arms.

Another loud drum beat sounded in the air, vibrating through their bodies and shaking the earth. Another repetition. The sound took on a steady pace, broken up by staccato flashes of lightning that encircled them, singeing the sand until they were standing within a circle of molten silicate. It bubbled and hissed as the temperature soared. Standing in the center, Maryam and Hasad clung tighter still to each other. He wrapped his arms around her as if to protect her from the heat with his body. Maryam panted, trying to catch her breath as the fire around them burned.

"Hasad!" she yelled against the din, but she received no response.

His hands were clammy against her arms and she felt faint as the temperature continued to rise. The sound continued, and as the noise increased in volume, the lightning cracks came closer together.

"Hasad!" Maryam screamed, terrified.

He held her tight to him, strength returning to his limbs as the desperation of the situation sank in.

I will not lose another! Rebekah! Recai! I will not lose Maryam too!

The ground shook beneath them and the ring of molten sand surrounding them boiled and spat as it sank into the sand, melting its way deep into the ground. Above, the sky sparked and a fire burst just as the ground gave out beneath them.

Maryam screamed as they slid beneath the surface. Sand filled in behind them, closing over them rapidly as they slid into the belly of the earth. Blackness swallowed them and directed them along a sliding path. Hasad clenched his eyes shut and held the screaming woman with determination.

The reverberating booming which had preceded their descent pulsed until it bled together into one continuous resonance. The sand thrust them downward into the darkness. Hasad no longer knew in what direction they slid. Maryam's screams stopped when the sand began filling her mouth. She buried her head in Hasad's neck.

The sand slowed and for a while their bodies slid along with the sand until they were falling again. With a painful thud they landed on a stone floor. Hasad stood in the darkness, keeping a hand on Maryam so as not to lose her in the blackness.

"Saqar!" Maryam coughed out.

She trembled in the black cavern, cold slick stone beneath her as she prostrated before Allah. The direction of Mecca was hidden here in this void of hell, but she would repent.

Allaahu Akbar . . .

Allaahu Akbar . . .

"Get up!" Hasad commended, grabbing the terrified girl by the arm. "Pray in your head; your God doesn't want you to die down here. We have to find a way out."

"We've been sent here in punishment!" Maryam sobbed, her faith rocked. She believed she'd been following the laws of Islam, but if she was trapped underground at the gates of hell, perhaps she'd been wrong all along.

"This isn't punishment. There's no hell that smells like mold and chills you with wet air."

Maryam sniffed as she stood in the dark, feeling the warmth of Hasad's steady hand on her arm.

"No, hell is fire and we are the fuel..." Blinking with the hope that her eyes would adjust, Maryam sighed with a shaky breath. "Then where are we?"

"I don't know."

The dank air surrounded them, creeping into every space, saturating them with its presence. With a hand in front of him and the other tightly gripping Maryam's, Hasad stepped into the thick air, blindly searching for a wall. Slick rock met his hand, the humidity in the air leaving a moist residue on everything. He pulled Maryam along so she stayed tight against the wall behind him as he followed it forward. At least now he had a point of reference in the abyss.

Each step spiked his anxiety. There could be a break in the ground, a well to fall into or a rise he might slam a shin against. Getting injured in the unknown void would mean death, and he had Maryam to think about. His usual confidence was tempered by caution as he probed the darkness.

The two walked for hours. Time suspended in the underground labyrinth. Hasad convinced himself more than once that he had been walking in a circle the entire time, leading them nowhere. Maryam was quiet as she recited verses of the Qu'ran in her mind to steady her nerves and fight the mounting terror of blindness.

"Stop," Hasad whispered. His voice did not travel far; the oppressive moisture absorbed the sound.

"Do you see something?"

Maryam gripped his shoulder from behind, straining to see over him.

"There's a turn, come on."

He moved again, leading them sharply to the left along a wall that turned with a precision indicating it was made by man, not nature. Just ahead, the faint dripping sound of water and a flicker of soft light appeared.

"A djinn?" Maryam asked, suspecting trickery in the sudden oasis.

"Nonsense. Fairy tales," Hasad snorted before pulling her forward to investigate.

As they neared the sound, light spread out and illuminated a dark cavern with holes in the walls from floor to ceiling, trapping them in what loosely resembled a beehive. The light glowed from behind a waterfall running along the back wall. Water pooled on the floor and disappeared into a crevasse in the rock beneath them, disappearing into the earth.

"Water!" Maryam called, letting go of Hasad and running over to put her hands into the flow. "Hasad, there's something... There's nothing on the other side!"

"Not a wall?"

"No."

He stepped up next to her and reached a hand into the stream, drenching his shirt. Open air greeted him. Groping blindly, Hasad found nothing in the space behind the wall of water.

"The light is coming from here," he muttered, kneeling down and feeling for solid ground. Stepping into this watery gate only to fall into some further cavern in the earth was not in his plan, although no plan of his had gone according to the agenda his entire life. Being here in the first place was proof of that.

Hasad pulled his hand back and looked up at Maryam. He nodded before standing, taking her hand, and stepping into the unknown.

The water fell fast and soaked their clothing. It filled their shoes and weighed down their clothes. Maryam pulled the soaked *hijab* off her head so it could dry. In her heart, Hasad had already become family; there could be no shame here.

On the other side a dim light filled another large cavern lined with carved holes. Obviously man-made, the openings were each identical in shape and size. Releasing Hasad's hand, Maryam went to investigate, leaning into the darkness of the nearest opening.

"What are you doing? Let's get out of here." Hasad said as he stepped toward the light, peering into the dim illumination, desperate to find something that would give him a sense of where they were.

"Hold on, I want to... I want to see what's in here." Maryam's curiosity outweighed her fear.

"Careful, spiders and scorpions love places like this."

"There are no bugs down here. Scorpions don't like places with no food. It's fine."

It was dark and dank within the opening. She reached in slowly with her hand until she found something to hold onto. Maryam pulled at it, heard a cracking sound and pulled back her hand, retrieving a gray bone. With a scream she threw the bone back into the hole and shuddered, looking around them. She backed away, falling against Hasad.

"This whole place... it's graves!"

He held her shoulders and scanned the cavern.

"Not graves. This is some kind of catacomb . . . but those are on the other side of the city, near the river." A voice spoke from deep in the darkness.

"These are the ancient catacombs from before the Anatolians, before the ancient city of Hasankeyf. Very few people know what's down here, and now, today, you are my second visitors."

Stepping out into the room so his image was no longer obscured by the light behind him came Imam Al-Bashir.

"

arya!"

Her uncle's voice rang out from her main rooms, making her jump. Her afternoon cup of coffee slipped from her hands and fell over the railing, speeding down to smash into whatever it met in the street below.

She took a steadying breath and fought against the constriction in her chest that seemed to be trying to kill her with terror. She had been waiting for him to arrive, but the reality of his presence shook her confidence. Looking out into the desert she saw another flash of lightning, and reminded herself that pure power is afraid of nothing.

The oversized silhouette of the mayor greeted Darya when she walked back into her apartment, the lightning storm in the desert forgotten in the angry fire of his eyes. His jowly face twisted with contempt.

"Darya," he greeted curtly, the vein in his soft forehead bulging.

"Uncle."

She approached him with a straight back, holding his eyes with her own. She would not be cowed; this city was hers now.

"I sent your housekeeper home. We could use some privacy."

"Could we?" Darya raised an eyebrow in challenge. "I have nothing to say that can't be overheard."

"No?"

"No."

"Darya..." the mayor began, clenching his fists. He stood with a wide stance and despite his lack of training in recent years, his body was still strong beneath his layers of fat. He held his chest high and overwhelmed the room with his presence. Darya did not retreat.

"You've gone too far," he began through gritted teeth. "How long?"

"How long what, Mahmet? How long have I been stealing your money or how long have I been advancing my own interests through the RTK? I've been playing father against son, exposing you all for the worms you are, as weak as the weakest woman in your company. Either way, it's been just long enough to make sure you're out of time."

Darya's smile was slow and dangerous. She leaned against the desk, hoping its solid structure would support her shaking legs. There was no time for weakness now.

Mahmet Yilmaz stared at his niece. He moved slowly, placing one foot carefully in front of the other. He did not speak as he approached, and Darya did not look away. She held his eyes instead of bowing her head. She was done deferring to men just because they expected it. She stood before her uncle with her hair uncovered and wearing the designer jeans she had bought in a moment of rebellion.

The impact of his hand against her face was sudden. Darya cried out as she fell over the top of her desk, the corner digging painfully into her side. Papers scattered before the heavy-set man whose chest heaved with the exhilaration of violence.

"You've gone too far," he repeated as she righted herself before him.

"You've lost," Darya seethed. "You have nothing, you are nothing. You can hit me if you want, but you'll never get any of it back."

Mahmet loomed over her, his breath reeking of cigarettes and corruption.

"Your father would be so ashamed," was the last thing he said before raising his hand again.

The first strike had been open-handed, a slap to remind a woman of her place. Now he struck with a closed fist. Darya's head jerked back, her body following the movement until she lay upon the ground. Mahmet's face was red as he panted before delivering the first kick to her abdomen. With powerful legs he repeatedly kicked her in the stomach.

She swallowed a scream as the impact ripped through her. She would not show him weakness. Fury battled with the trained child inside that told her to apologize, to give in to him. Her body begged for the beating to end, but pride would not concede.

"Uncle!" she panted, unable to stay silent as he kicked her again in the thigh before reaching down and wrenching her body up before him.

"You think you're a man? You think you can tell me what to do? Who's in charge? You are nothing. You are a deceiver, a whore! You are nothing!" Mahmet spat the words out, shaking her.

"No…" she keened, blood dripping from her nose and lip, the pain in her abdomen overwhelming. She had been vain. She thought she could win. Nothing in this world had ever given her reason to believe it was possible for her to have something of her own. It was impossible to think she would ever own anything without a man's name attached to it or be regarded as someone worthy of respect, and still she had fought for a life she controlled. She should have known better.

Mahmet threw Darya back against the glass doors leading out to the balcony. The curtains parted as she collided, allowing in a sparking flash of lightning. Darya fell to the floor, her body screaming for reprieve from the abuse. Mahmet approached his niece with a sneer and the glint of evil in his eye. "You're just a woman acting like a man. Give me a reason why I shouldn't have you dismembered and left in the desert for vultures to eat."

Placing his swollen hand on his belt, Mahmet unzipped his pants.

Darya scrambled away from him, pushing her burning muscles to help her escape. The voice inside her, where she thought of this man as a father, screamed, but her lips remained sealed shut. Wide-eyed and full of horror, she shook her head no.

Mahmet rounded the desk, cutting off any escape for Darya's crawling figure. He pulled back his leg and delivered a cracking blow to her face. Screams filled the air as her bones shattered and Darya's body flew against the wall before sliding limply to the floor.

Through a bloody veil of pain, Darya accepted the horror of her position. Mahmet intended to show her her place one way or another. Bile rose in her mouth and she gagged. Leaning over, Darya vomited onto the floor what little food she had in her system.

Mahmet's laugh was full of madness and hatred. It was the sound of pure evil.

"Stay down."

Mahmet spat his words so violently Darya expected them to have a physical impact.

"No."

"You've learned nothing."

Lifting his leg he lashed out at her again, but Darya's fear and devastation turned to fury. Despite the pain that coursed through her entire body she slid out of his range, making him stumble into the wall.

"Bitch."

He reached out and grabbed her hair, pulling her up to her knees while yanking some of her silky locks free from her skull.

"I gave you everything, I gave you this home," he pulled her by the hair to slam her face into the wall. "I gave you work."

He yanked hard again, pulling her on her side as he stormed toward her desk. Darya frantically crawled and pushed off with her feet in an attempt to keep up with his pace, the pain from her scalp slicing deep within her. When he reached the desk he lifted her up to her feet and scowled directly into her overflowing eyes.

"You have no understanding of your role. Today you'll learn."

Mahmet released his niece's hair before turning violently and slamming her face down onto the keyboard of her computer. He pushed her forward, knocking the monitor off the desk with her head. Her hipbones cried out from the impact of the desk's edge. Darya tried to push up and stand, screaming. But every time she did, Mahmet would use his fist, his hand, his elbow to punish the back of her head.

"Be still and learn your lesson. You're no pure virgin, you'll never marry. You might as well be good for something," he growled into her neck, leaning over so his massive bulk pinned her against the desk.

Her hands clawed at the desk and her feet sought leverage to help catapult her out of her uncle's grasp.

"Always in pants. Always so strong, so opinionated. You flaunt your disobedience."

"No!"

Flailing, Darya knocked over the remaining items on her desk, searched for something to hold on to, to help her get away. The scissors in her right top drawer were too far away to reach.

Mahmet's sweat dripped down from him, landing on Darya's back as he gripped the back of her neck, pushing her face harder against the desk. When she stopped struggling he released his hold slightly and leaned over her, forcing his oversized paw beneath her until he held her breast.

"Mahmet, please!"

"Yes, please. Yes, beg for forgiveness, for leniency. That is how a woman wins a fight, by submitting to her superior. Hell is full of women who forget their place!"

Mahmet stood up and wrenched her around, flipping her body so her back slammed on the desk.

"I submit nothing," Darya seethed through clenched teeth.

"You submit to me."

The sun began to set in the distance, leaving the penthouse dark and warm. Mahmet's drooping jowls shone with sweat in the twilight. Pain shot through Darya when Mahmet slapped her, but she did not cry out. Her mind stilled as a plan solidified. She took advantage of the space between them and kicked him in the groin before reaching into the drawer.

"You stupid bitch," he seethed. Once the tears in his eyes subsided, he back-handed her, throwing her body back against the desk. Her face throbbed when the impact of the blow registered, but she kept her hands clenched to her chest.

When she sat up, the mayor sought her eyes, failing to notice the glimmer of the falling sun reflecting off the metal scissors. Darya tensed and struck true in the center of his left eye.

Mahmet screamed as she pushed the scissors through his orb, letting the viscous fluid explode across her face. His shock propelled him sideways, flailing like an animal. Instinct had not given him the sense to defend himself and Darya followed, thrusting the scissors deeper until the tip pierced the back of his eye and slipped into the soft tissue of his brain.

Mayor Mahmet Yilmaz slumped to the floor, his eye oozing blood and ocular fluid. He laid spasming on the ground in the final animalistic movements of his life.

Darya mounted his flabby torso, screams of pain and anger filling the air. She wrenched the scissors from his face, falling off-center with the effort. An ululation broke from her as she brought the scissors down to his throat and chest again and again.

"I submit to nothing," she spat, breathless, staring at the bloody remains of her uncle lying beneath her.

Heart frozen, she stood and walked to the desk on shaking legs. She picked up her phone and dialed the one person she knew she could trust. The only family she'd ever really had.

"Isik, I need you," was all she said before her heart thawed and she collapsed under the horror of what she had done.

PART 5

"AS FOR THOSE WHO BELIEVE AND DO RIGHT ACTIONS, THE ALL-MERCIFUL WILL BESTOW HIS LOVE ON THEM."

Surah Maryam, 96

Imam Al-Bashir's pace was brisk. Motion-sensing lights glowed as he traveled with the young girl and the old man through the tunnels. His loose-fitting pants hung down to his shoes and dragged along the dirty ground, although the rest of him was immaculately kept. With modest clothing and a trimmed but full beard, Imam Al-Bashir was the picture of the devoted Ulama.

Maryam struggled to keep up with him; the ground was uneven and rocky, and her clothes weighed heavily from her frame. The water squished under her toes in the shoes she wore, the dampness of her clothes contrasting with the arid change in the air. The humidity had dissipated and now the familiar taste of heat and sand filled her senses. Her nerves were frayed, but she was recovering. Having the Imam there to lead the way gave her a tremendous sense of relief.

Behind her, Hasad's breathing was labored and raspy, making the nurse in her worry about the old man's ability to maintain the Imam's pace. Maryam knew Hasad was proud. He'd rather wheeze than have her ask to slow down on his account, and as long as he didn't seem to be in pain or dizzy she wasn't worried about his heart. So she kept her head down and her eyes on the feet of the man leading them back to civilization.

When the path began to even out the Imam slowed. Hasad stumbled at the back of the group at the change in the terrain, but he regained his footing quickly. The exertion shone on his forehead, but his eyes were as critical as always.

"Imam?" Maryam ventured.

The man cocked his head in her direction and nodded without breaking stride. The dim light was brighter now. In the distance she could see a warm glow reaching along the pocked walls of the tunnel.

"Where are we?"

"The ancient catacombs of the Tigris," he replied.

"Bunk," Hasad spat. "The tombs are on the other side of the city."

Imam Al-Bashir stopped his forward press and turned to face the unlikely crusaders following him. "How exactly did you get down here?"

"First, tell us where the hell we are," Hasad demanded, earning a grimace from Maryam.

"I'm sorry," she began but the Imam laughed.

"I have told you. You're in the catacombs of the Tigris River. Not the River as you know it now, not the river as it flowed when Hasankeyf was still resplendent. This," the Imam gestured with one hand to the walls around them, "was once the underground river that flowed so long ago we can't calculate."

"How is it here? I've never heard of it," Maryam inquired, looking at the Imam's dark eyes in the warmth of the lights mounting on the cave walls.

He smiled, showing white teeth beneath his tidy mustache.

"Let's go to your friend. I assume that's why you're here. Then you can tell me who you are."

"Our friend?"

"Yes, a man came this way earlier, covered in sand. He sent me to find you, he said you would be here, and you are! Ya Allah, I've never seen anyone come through here, and now three in one day."

"Recai!" Maryam exclaimed, turning to Hasad.

"He's not dead then."

"No, not at all, he's upstairs, praying. Come, let's get above ground."

"And then you'll tell us how there's an entire system of tunnels down here no one's ever heard of," Hasad insisted.

"Yes, I'll tell you that as well."

Imam Al-Bashir led them farther along in the system of caves and tunnels. The stone changed from damp to dry until the walls themselves ached for water as much as the lost pair following behind the Imam. Each turn revealed something new; the color of the clay walls, the taste of heat. Their feet no longer sloshed through puddles but dragged sand along as they shuffled to keep up.

Maryam counted the changes up and filed them away. Later, when she was in her own home, she could think about what she had seen and heard. Now her focus was on the straight back of the Imam.

Soon the walls began to resemble the earthen structures of the ancient city that stood here generations before Elih was born. Maryam had visited the Tombs of the Tigris when she first moved to the city. Tourism was for tourists, but the sites were exciting nonetheless. The city sat low in the riverbed of the diverted river, filled with vendors selling everything from pets to spices to tailored men's suits.

The bustling marketplace was the only part of Elih that felt like home to her. The small town she grew up in was filled with colorful cloths and food sold from stands and right out of kitchen windows. Living near the sea meant there were always tourists willing to spend money—Americans curious about Turkey, but not willing to venture into the wild inland cities. Her brothers had made their living guiding tours and selling things they gathered from smaller, poorer villages.

It wasn't so long ago that all of Elih had smelled of rose soap and saffron, but that ended when the RTK came into power. Now the only remaining glimpse of the Turkey she had grown up in resided in the ruins of Hasankeyf.

The Imam stopped in front of a sharp-turning passageway leading away from the main tunnel.

"Here, this is how we get to the mosque."

Hasad straightened and coughed before looking at Maryam uncomfortably.

"Imam, my friend, he is a Jew. Is he welcome as well?"

Imam Al-Bashir stared at her for a moment, his eyes dark and impenetrable, before turning to face Hasad.

"We are all sons of Ibrahim here."

He bowed with a kind smile to the dirty man who simply panted for breath then nodded his bow in return.

While the unlikely trio made their trek through the city's underbelly, Darya stood by the door to her penthouse with the dripping scissors still in her hand. She kept vigil over her uncle's body, which lay belly up on her office rug like a whale come to shore to die.

The sound of a key sliding into the lock of the front door screamed within her head, the deafening click threatening to break her sanity. The knob turned slowly and a knot tightened inside her chest, pulling her insides together into a claustrophobic vice. Her heart ached with pressure, desperate to flee the hold her hatred had on it.

"Darya?" Isik called in a loud whisper before opening the door farther. "Darya, Sister, it's me."

Isik stepped through the front door into the abandoned foyer. No housekeeper or security guard rushed out to stop him. The apartment was eerily calm. Inching farther into the opulent home, a deepening sense of urgency struck him. The sound of her voice on the phone, the deathly calm of the apartment, none of it added up and he feared for her—and himself.

"You called and I'm here," he continued, his voice muted by the thickness of pain in the air. "I'm here to help you, Sister."

Rounding the corner into the main room of her living quarters, Isik saw Darya, covered in blood.

"Darya!" he cried, rushing to her.

With still eyes and a glacier gaze, Darya lifted and pointed the tip of the scissors at her half-brother's throat. The hatred he saw in her look made him recoil well before he registered the physical threat.

"What happened?"

With a nod, Darya gestured to where the mayor lay in his own blood, bile, and urine. Isik approached the body cautiously, certain of its earthly death but superstitious about the spirits that might still linger. Whatever happened here did not happen without the devil's hand.

Behind the desk Darya's overturned chair was lying in the pool of vomit she had spit up earlier. A streak of blood ran down the wall, and the curtain was pulled off its precariously hanging rod. Isik's stomach lurched to see his uncle's pants pulled down below his knees, his penis severed.

"Did you do this?" Isik asked without looking up, his hardened shell taking in the scene before him without emotion.

"He deserved it," Darya responded flatly.

"No doubt." Isik stood and faced his sister. "Are you all right?"

"You mean do I still have my honor?" she scorned.

"You lost that years ago, and I have no interest in honor for you or myself. But are you hurt? Do you need... something?"

Tears welled behind Darya's eyes and pushed against the layer of ice that had formed over her pupils. They would stay trapped, prisoners of her hate along with her heart.

Stillness was her only response. Nothing was all right. Nothing would ever again be all right. She bled from her face, her mouth, her nose. She bled from injuries seen and unseen. She bled until she exsanguinated, nothing left to keep her frozen heart beating. Hate became the only thing keeping her alive.

Recai knelt on the tile floor of the mosque, his head bent in supplication, forehead against cold tiles. Around him sand gathered, drawn to him and his newly found connection with his homeland. Slowly the earthen grit moved along an unseen breeze until it landed near him. Small piles of sand rose as he supplicated himself before Allah.

With hands flat on the ground he recited from the Qu'ran silently, the words flowing through his mind like a breeze, refreshing and effortless: *But those who wronged among them changed the words to a statement other than that which had been said to them. So we sent upon them a punishment from the sky for the wrong that they were doing*

Earlier today Recai had been swallowed by the earth, cleansed by the harshness of the sand. His feet had moved independently, drawn through the darkness until he found himself standing at the threshold of decision.

"Are you here to pray?" the Imam had asked in the deep, smooth voice of a cantor.

"I don't know."

"Best then to try, whatever your reason for being here. Prayer can help you find the way."

"I came through the sand."

The Imam had stiffened.

"Through the sand?"

"The sand and the tunnels, I found my way...but my friends," he looked up at the Imam with

*urgent revelation. "I know they will look for me. My
friends will be lost."*

"Ya Allah!"

"You go find them…I'll pray."

Recai now breathed in the sunlight surrounding him, its
purity and heat filling him with purpose. He had not been a
devout man, he had not always been a good man, but he believed
the truth of the message sent to him in the desert. Those who had
perverted the teachings of the Prophet Mohammed and the very
word of Allah would be punished. Nothing he did with all of his
money would make a difference until something changed.

He finished his silent prayer, whispering "Ameen," before
standing and turning toward the inner rooms of the Mosque. Further
inside the Imam was talking in hushed tones, refusing to allow
anyone to disturb him. Even the people he'd been sent to retrieve.

"I don't want a glass of water, or to sit down. I want to
see Recai."

Recai smiled hearing the sound of Hasad's annoyed voice as
he rounded the corner to the office. His gruff, direct ways were
strangely comforting in a world filled with politics and conspiracies.

Hasad paced, wiping his hands on his dusty and stained
pants over and over. His stance was hunched, making him look older
than usual; worry had aged him. Eventually, he stopped pacing and
stood behind Maryam, his protective aura encompassing her. She sat
quietly on a low stool, her back sagging so that she slumped forward.
With her hands in her lap she looked blankly at the Imam as he
explained the hidden tunnels they had discovered.

"Hasankeyf is an ancient city. The ruins have told us
about our history as Turks and Muslims. But it's not the oldest
discovery. They tell you in school about the Hasankeyf, the rock
fortress and how it existed before men were men."

Recai lingered outside the office, curious about the story. If he
entered the room, the conversation would change from the historic to
the present, and he sensed a lesson within the Imam's words.

"Allah is the creator of everything: the animals, the plants, the worlds within worlds. Allah is the creator of causes, and he alone creates the effect. When he made man out of clay, he breathed life into us and gave us a soul, elevating us above the other creatures on the earth. This is truth. This is the message the Prophet, *Salla Allahu 'Alaihi Wa Sallam*, gave to us.

"In the cliff walls of Hasankeyf and in the mountains of Diyaribira Tepesi remains have been found that show evidence that there were people here, long ago. Different enough from us to not be men, but close enough to not be animal. Science and religion met in the ruins of Turkey and began a series of questions no one could answer."

"Evolution," Hasad interjected. "That's just evolution. Any toddler knows that a fish crawled out of the water and grew into a person. We don't need a lesson in common sense."

"Hasad!" Maryam exclaimed, lifting her eyes to the Imam in apology.

"Yes," the Imam laughed. "For most believers evolution is truth. For many it's not. The Ulama is divided. Some believe science can't be refuted while others believe it is a trick of nature. Either way, the day the first man awoke and Allah breathed life into him was the beginning of humanity. We are all the sons of Adam.

"In the tunnels beneath us, there are graves filled with men, those who came before men, animals, and women—all intermixed. These graves travel along the underground from below Hasankeyf out into the mountains. We've lost the path under Gurabala Tepesi; the mountain is just too dense and rocky to continue with our limited resources."

"That's… you're keeping this from the people?" Hasad asked.

"Yes."

"That's criminal! That's history!"

Hasad gripped the back of Maryam's chair with his scar-ridden arthritic fingers.

"In a way I agree with you. But the Imams who discovered it felt it was too dangerous to tell anyone. The revelation would cause many to lose faith in Allah's word, calling the story of our creation into question. They did not trust the people to see how scientific proof and faith can exist simultaneously, and now the secret has been kept so long I fear it would cause more harm than good to reveal it."

"Men and non-men? Living together?" Maryam's voice cut through their debate as she saw the theological problem before her.

"Perhaps. At the very least, they died together."

"It doesn't matter," Recai spoke as he stepped into the office, eliciting a gasp from Maryam. "Allah tells us to take care of the orphans and needy, to tend to the animals and the earth. Men or not-men, we're still commanded to wish for them what we wish for ourselves."

"Recai!" Hasad charged the younger man and grasped him roughly, pulling his body close. "You are the most difficult, ornery child I've ever known. I don't know why I've been cursed to watch over you."

The older man pulled away, salty tracks running down his dirty face.

"I know Hasad. I'll do better."

Recai smiled and kissed the older man affectionately on the cheek.

Maryam sat frozen. Her body vibrated with relief and stress until tears spilled over. Hiding her face in her hands, she sobbed, her disheveled hijab concealing her completely.

"Maryam!" Recai released Hasad's embrace and rushed to his distraught friend. "Maryam, *fistik*, no…"

He reached for her hands, but she would not release herself into him and he would not cross the barrier of appropriateness to touch her.

"Leave her," Hasad suggested. "Sometimes women just need to cry."

"Please, look at me," Recai continued. "I'm fine. I'm here, and you're safe."

"I know that," she sniffed.

Recai waited as Al-Bashir and Hasad looked on uncomfortably until Maryam released a shaky sigh.

"You are in so much trouble," she said lowering her hands and looking at Recai's green eyes. "You are in so much trouble. You're going to wish the earth had swallowed you up and kept you in its belly!"

Recai's face split into a broad smile, making Maryam scowl before pushing him as hard as she could. Her blow offset his center of balance, making him land hard on the ornate Kashmir rug covering the floor.

"So much trouble!"

Maryam stood and stormed out of the office toward the entrance of the mosque. Recai got up, bent his head, and followed her out.

"Maryam!"

She stormed on without glancing behind her.

"Maryam! Why are you angry?"

He reached out and placed a hand on her arm to draw her attention to him. When she stopped walking, he pulled his hand back and stepped in front of her.

"What is it?"

"Hasad is right," she replied.

She stopped walking. Her hands shook as she adjusted her headscarf before looking up at Recai.

"You are stupid and impetuous and infuriating."

"I am," he chuckled low beneath his breath, holding her eyes with a smile.

"I was so scared," she admitted.

"I know."

Recai's voice was soft as he relaxed, sure that now she would talk to him.

"I don't know what time it is. I don't know what day it is. I'm exhausted, I'm starving, and I'm probably late for work. And it's all because you felt the need to drive into a sandstorm in the middle of the night like some lunatic jihadi storming Jerusalem!"

She paused, and Recai allowed her a moment to gather her thoughts so the wool of their meaning could be woven into words.

"And I was worried about you. I barely know you, and here I am looking like a drowned rat covered in muck after searching for you!"

"Maryam, I am sorry."

"I believed in you, and this is what happens!"

Recai took a step away from her and ran a rough hand across his face. He was tired, so tired of trying to understand what Allah wanted from him. The effort aged him twenty years, every day.

"I've been lost since Rebekah died."

Maryam stilled. This was the first time Recai had spoken of Hasad's daughter. Tears pooled in the corners of his eyes.

"I don't understand why I survived being left in the desert, only to witness… and live…. I tried to lose myself, but the city drew me home. And since I've been back it's like there's nothing I can do. My father's company is falling apart. Money is missing and no one can explain it. I have no real friends left; they've all left for overseas, or were never friends in the first place. Nothing I've tried to do has worked. I've made no difference, and now I've upset you, one of the only people I feel that I can actually trust."

"You're wrong, Recai." Maryam's eyes remained on the ground, her voice hushed but confident. "You saved Hasad from doing something stupid. He came to the city looking for revenge, but now he has you, and me, and something to live for."

Recai exhaled loudly, begrudgingly accepting her point.

"And you rescued Sabiha. She's safe now! And Fahri brought in someone else. What you did changed him…. You should hear the nurses at the hospital talking about what you did, about what it would be like to not feel afraid every time we went outside alone. You started something important."

"I didn't want it. I don't want to be important. I just . . . I'm so tired, Maryam."

Recai closed his eyes and leaned against the wall, the hours of sleeplessness, the weeks of confusion, the years of mourning weighing him down. They filled his shoes and clung to his clothes, dragging him down to the floor.

"I can't do anything about that."

She approached, keeping a respectable distance, but close enough to show she trusted him and cared about him.

"But whatever happened out there in the desert last night, whatever pulled Hasad and me into those tunnels, whatever keeps you alive despite your insistence on trying to kill yourself through stupidity, it thinks you are important."

Recai looked up at her. She spoke the truth; he didn't want to hear it, yet his own prayer had shown him the will of Allah: *We sent upon them a punishment from the sky for the wrong that they were doing.*

The shop's door opened, setting off the welcoming jingle of the small bells hanging above. Abdullah looked up from the counter as three RTK officers entered, smiling in the evening sun.

He hid his comic book beneath the counter and ran a hand through his haphazard curls as the officers milled through the far aisle, speaking in hushed tones. Abdullah tried to look less like a disheveled single man who lived with his parents and more like someone the RTK would respect.

"Assalamu Alaikum," a burly officer with a fistful beard greeted, approaching the counter with a bag of jerky in his hand.

"Walaikum as salaam," he replied.

"You're Aziz's brother."

The guard placed a bag down on the counter and looked behind him. The others were still grazing toward the back of the store. Abdullah glanced at the officer's gun holster slung over his uniform, unclasped.

"Yes. He'll be here later. Do you know him?"

"He usually has something for us," the RTK officer announced.

He leaned closer to Abdullah, his bushy eyebrows pulled low over his deep-set eyes.

"Do you know anything about that?"

"I… I don't," Abdullah stuttered. "But I can look in the back, see if there's anything there."

The other guards were making their way toward the counter, boots heavy against the linoleum floor. Abdullah was not used to having the RTK in the store; they usually stayed away. He was awed and terrified of their presence.

"Done?" a taller guard with close-trimmed hair and a clean-shaven face asked, slapping the larger officer standing at the counter on the shoulder.

"Aziz isn't here."

"Kahretsin!"

"No, listen, I'll go look," Abdullah insisted.

He stumbled off of his chair and lifted the counter opening that separated him from the shop.

"Is it a package? Or, what size is it?"

He stood in front of the muscled commandos, his foppish hair and wrinkled clothes more fitting for a child than a grown man running a store. He squared his shoulders as the taller officer appraised him.

"All right, there's usually an envelope. It isn't big, but it's heavy. It should say 'For Aliya' on it. You get that for us."

"Okay, I'll find it."

Abdullah skittered back to the office, making sure to avoid bumping into the third officer, who was assessing the limited ice cream selection in the freezer section.

The back room was cluttered as usual. Papers lay scattered on top of the desk. His father's version of bookkeeping meant stuffing every piece of paper into an envelope and then piling the envelopes on his desk. The financials of the business overflowed onto the floor in a steady stream of purchase orders, receipts, and shipping invoices.

"For Aliya...for Aliya..." he mumbled to himself.

Abdullah searched, going through each of the envelopes on the desk. None of them were labeled in any way. He pulled out the drawers, searched the bags on the floor that were full of bills and used checkbooks. The computer sat silent on the secretary's desk against the wall, boxes of toilet paper stacked on top of it.

"Damn it!"

Abdullah searched again, frantic to find whatever his brother had for the RTK. He was sure it wasn't legal, but who better to be in league with than the RTK? Selfishly, he wanted whatever his brother had for himself. Maybe if he had more money, more respect, Maryam would rethink his ill-timed proposal.

Leaning against the cases of soda lining the far wall, Abdullah was about to give up hope. Back in the corner there was one more place to look. A filing cabinet that held the deed to the building, the insurance policies, his parent's marriage certificate, and every legal document his father wanted to keep safe. They were all back there locked inside a fire box.

Squeezing himself through the narrow space, Abdullah stepped over the packing boxes he was supposed to have broken down and hauled to the dumpster yesterday. The florescent light flickered overhead.

Wrenching the ancient file cabinet drawer open, Abdullah found the key for the fire box taped inside the file labeled "Ballet Classes." He shoved the drawer closed with his arm and bent down to the bottom drawer. There was just enough room to open it and unlock the small safe.

Inside, on top of the family's documents was a thick envelope labeled "For Aliya."

At home, in the comfort of his own space, Recai slept. His feet were dirty against the Egyptian cotton of his sheets, and his soiled clothes lay on the floor in disarray. Exhausted and confused, Recai escaped reality into the realm of dreams.

Maryam had left for her apartment after accompanying him home from their strange meeting place. She made him swear to Allah he would call her before going on any more suicidal adventures. Hasad retreated to his own room, spent. His body ached and creaked more with each step. Tomorrow they would regroup, refocus—but for now they all just needed to rest.

As they slept, dust sparkled in the evening air. Sand particles slowly drifted from atop doorways and between minute cracks in the wall. Sailing along the current of the breeze, sand migrated toward its home. Like recognizes like and is drawn together by the comfort of similarity. Along the floor a dusting of sand was gathering in Recai's room.

Tossing with visions from the dreamscape, Recai's arm fell from the side of his bed, reaching down into the soft sand below. Its warmth and comfort calmed his unseen fears and lulled him deeper into slumber.

Night crashed against the horizon, leaving the sky over the desert defenseless against the piercing starlight. The daylight hibernation of nocturnal creatures ended, and the fight for survival continued on under the cloak of black. Sand moved along the dunes, shifting beneath the footsteps of nomadic wanderers and hunting scorpions. Sand drifted along unseen waves, creating and destroying its own landscape.

Sand lay in wait, gently piling around the resting form of the man the desert chose to save.

Abdullah was elated when Maryam came into the store the next morning. He feared she'd been avoiding him since their last conversation. His palms were moist from the heat of the air despite the fan pointing directly at him behind the counter, and his excitement at seeing her made his heart pound.

Their last nighttime encounter hadn't gone the way he had dreamed it would. In his mind, she had been delighted to see him, willing to talk to him, maybe accompany him to one of the coffee shops or bars open late. He should have known better, should have seen the hesitation in her eyes when he approached. But he was too focused on the possibilities within his mind to see the reality of what played out before him.

"Are you working today?" he asked casually when she approached.

"Yes, well…" she indicated the scrubs she was wearing over her thin, long sleeved shirt and hijab.

"Oh, well, I didn't know if… I mean you could have just gotten home or something," he stuttered; wiping his hands on his pants he wished there was air-conditioning so he wasn't sweaty as he spoke to her.

"Are there any sandwiches left?"

"Yes! Oh, yes there are a few! I think I have one more egg and cheese if you want it."

"No bacon?" she teased.

"If it were up to me, for you, I would serve pork."

Abdullah's smile was open and broad. She was speaking to him, joking even. He couldn't have been happier if he'd won a million lira. Perhaps he hadn't ruined things. *In'shallah*, he would have the chance to try to win her heart again.

He pulled a sandwich out of the insulated bag his mother packed every morning and placed it in a paper bag with an orange. Maryam dropped money on the counter, but when he set the bag in front of her, he pushed it back.

"No, you take this. I was too forward the other night." Abdullah lowered his eyes and ran a nervous hand through his curls. "I owe you an apology."

She didn't respond immediately, and Abdullah worried that the hope he'd gleaned from her friendly demeanor this morning hadn't been misplaced.

"I'd be more comfortable if I paid," she said before taking the bag from the counter, leaving the money where it lay. Then, she spoke again.

"I'd like to be your friend. It's not haram; men and women can be friends, but maybe I've been wrong taking your gifts. I don't want to be someone who hurts you, Abdullah, so let me pay, and I'll accept your apology, and we can go back to being friends."

He groaned, his chest constricting tightly as he looked at her long fingers grasping the bag. Her smile was sad and kind. He wished he could reach out and touch her face.

"I don't want to be your friend. I want to show you I can be right for you." His voice pleaded despite his attempt to retain his dignity.

"You are a good man."

Maryam smiled sadly, fatigue showing in her flat eyes, their usual sparkle dimmed. Opening the paper bag, she pulled out the orange and placed it next to the money. Without glancing up, she turned away and walked out the door; the bells jingled with mocking lightness.

"Damn!" he swore, slapping his hand on the counter, sending the money she had left floating toward the floor. Laying his head on the counter, he cursed his luck, his life, his parents, Maryam, everything but himself. He knew he could be more than this. He had to find a way to show her.

Pulling from his pocket the piece of paper that the RTK officers had given him to pass on to his brother, Abdullah decided maybe it was time to be a part of something bigger than himself.

The sun set behind Isik on the loading dock as he pulled the metal side door open. Purple skies faded to gray, outlining his body with bruising colors. Shoving a wedge beneath it, he left the heavy door open.

Weeks of planning had gone into arranging this meeting. Convincing Darya to take action against their uncle hadn't been difficult, but the logistics of a coup had proven to be more complicated than he'd expected. The mayor had been announced missing already—now it was a question of salesmanship.

Stepping inside, he pulled a pack of cigarettes from his jeans pocket and plucked one out. After lighting it he inhaled deeply, allowing the tobacco to calm his nerves. He loved the soft high that a simple cigarette could induce and relished the quiet moment alone before his sister arrived.

Darya was a pain in his ass. She had everything he was denied; a family that claimed her, money, power. Fuck, he would have been happy just to have an apartment someone else paid for instead of sleeping in the room he rented from a distant cousin of his mother's. The entire place smelled like Jew, just like his childhood. The smell was as much to blame for his misfortune as his parentage.

He dragged on his cigarette while he surveyed the warehouse. Women's designer clothing filled racks and were dressed on mannequins. All the kinds of things you'd never see anyone wearing in public: miniskirts and halter-tops. "Couture fashion," Darya had told him. Stupid crap women put on under their abayas. The amount of money Turkish women spent on their hair, getting it cut and colored, along with the designer clothing was disgusting. No one would see it but their husbands, and who cares what wrapping you put on something when you already know what's underneath.

Isik switched on the office lights and pulled the floor lamp into the main space before flicking the last embers of his cigarette toward the door.

Darya had spent the day in her small office around the block, finishing paperwork or filing or whatever it was she did in there. There wasn't enough time to bother wasting it working like that, following other people's rules. Isik was more interested in making new rules, in building a new life for himself. The money and influence Darya had gathered was making this possible, but he knew no one would ever take her seriously. Just the idea of a woman in charge was like a bad joke. Elih wasn't Pakistan or India, and Darya wasn't some damn incarnation of Fatimah whom the people of the city could look up to as an icon of Islam.

Besides, since he'd ditched their loving uncle's body out in the desert for her, Darya had been quiet. She'd always been hard, tough. Her silence was more unsettling than her anger. Isik sat on one of the metal chairs scattered about and lit another cigarette, waiting for the lemmings to arrive.

Shadows climbed the walls like spirits from hell, witnesses to his treachery as the sound of his sister's heels clicked on the concrete stairs leading up to the loading dock. There was no going back now.

"Isik," she called, stepping into the gloomy room. Mannequins and their shadows circled the space.

"Yeah."

He tossed his half smoked cigarette onto the ground, where it smoldered near a pile of designer bras.

"Where are they? The meeting was supposed to start by now. I thought I was—"

She was cut off by the glint in his eye as he strode toward her. "Isik?"

"You've done everything right, everything you could," he began as he approached. "There's nothing more anyone could possibly do. You're smart, and you're beautiful."

"Where is everyone?" Darya asked again, refusing to cower, refusing to be afraid again.

"They'll be here, come on."

Turning his back on the only family who'd ever cared about his existence, Isik led the way to the small, windowless office.

"I've got a plan," he stated holding the door wider so that she could enter.

"Is it genius?" Darya asked. Her voice was flirtatious but her body cold and hard. Isik missed the sister his uncle had stolen from him.

"It is."

Isik stepped forward, forcing his sister to back away from him, farther into the room. He glanced down at her lips, wondering how she would taste. Would her mouth be as full of evil as his soul?

"I'm sorry, Darya, but this city just isn't yours to run."

Surprise flashed across her face as he pushed her into the office.

"Isik!" she screamed, recovering her footing and launching her body at the door. He pulled it closed before she reached it, leaving her trapped inside. Locking it from the outside, Isik released the breath he had been holding. Her screams were muffled behind the door, but he could still hear the fury in her voice.

Part of him wished it could be different, that he could keep his sister and the city. But she would never have given up; she was stubborn and blind to the realities of her world. Isn't that what made her such a ferocious fighter? But in the end she was too easy to deceive and he had the prejudice of an entire city on his side.

Poor Darya, he thought, *every time she thinks she's in control someone takes it from her.* He pocketed the only key to her cell with a smile.

He pulled a rack of clothing in front of the doorway, blocking it from anyone who entered before plugging in the large industrial fan sitting on the floor next to the office door. Her screams were dampened into silence. No one would ever know she was here.

Fahri Kana followed the other members of the Lion Division of the RTK along a back alley. They were off duty, but the brigade commander had called them together.

The RTK's concern over the man referred to as "The SandStorm" in *The Gazetesi* had diminished as the weeks went by and he remained in hiding. A fluke incident, a lone man overstepping his place for just a moment wasn't something to worry too much about.

As the group approached a loading dock, the commander stopped and turned to his men.

"You're the first to know, and I'm telling you because I trust you. You're my men, and I know you're the right men for this: The mayor's gone missing."

Silence vibrated around them as each processed the meaning of their leader's possible death. Excitement, fear, sadness, and relief floated into the air, creating an atmosphere of chaos.

"What happened?" one officer asked.

"Is he dead?" another questioned.

"It was from the inside, and we don't yet know who is responsible. But the RTK and city bank accounts are drained. Power's changing hands and it's starting tonight. I know someone who can pull the city together and keep our leadership strong even without Mayor Yilmaz. Tonight, the future's going to be decided. You can come in, or you can stay out here and melt in the heat with the rest of the city. No second chances."

Fahri's hands shook as he accepted an offered cigarette from the officer standing next to him. *What the hell is going on?*

Standing at the top of the stairs leading into the warehouse, a man appeared. He was tall, wearing tight-fitting jeans and a black t-shirt. His head was bare, and the tattoo on the side of his neck had eyes that peered out at Fahri as if it smelled his doubts.

"Come inside, there's a lot to do. My name is Dayar Yildirim."

He turned and walked into the dark mouth of the warehouse; the entire division followed him. Fahri blew out the smoke in his lungs and closed his eyes. He didn't want anything to do with this. But there was no way out. If he walked now, he'd be seen as a traitor. Quickly, before anyone could question why he hadn't followed, he flipped open his phone and sent a text to the number the nurse at the hospital had given him accompanied by a note that read "If you need us."

Texting with his thumbs, he squinted in the darkness for the right letters: *Safak Mh., 79071—Mayor is missing—come now.*

"Kana, are you coming?" Serge called out to him.

"Yeah, yeah, just texting Sabiha."

"Ever the lapdog, huh little man?"

"Yeah, well, at least I don't smell like an Arab," Fahri joked, his hands shaking as he stuffed his phone back into his pocket and strode inside.

At the hospital Maryam's phone vibrated in her scrubs' pocket, pulling her out of her thoughts. She was exhausted, sitting in the nurse's lounge, staring at the tile floor. It was one of the only places in the hospital where she could find some quiet. The doctors were not allowed in the lounge—it was open only to women staff members. As much as it made them angry when they couldn't demand the nursing staff's presence, they respected the need for separation of the sexes too much to barge in.

Her shift was slow. There was only an hour left before she'd be able to clock out and head home. Everything in her body ached for sleep. The past forty-eight hours had been exhausting. None of it made any sense. Secret catacombs, quicksand that delivered her to the Imam, Recai's strange role in all of this. She believed. She was faithful. But she had never seen a miracle before. Those things happened when The Prophet was alive, not now.

But then, her people had strayed so far from that path perhaps everything she had seen was a sign from Allah.

Taking her phone out of her pocket, Maryam leaned back and crossed her legs, a habit her mother had tried to break her of since she was a child, but the posture was comfortable. Fahri's message glowed on her screen.

Sitting up, she read the text again before dialing the phone.

Recai drove to the mosque in the Safak district. There he could leave his car, and the Imam would vouch for his presence at a special prayer meeting if anyone asked. When his phone had rung and Maryam told him of Fahri Kana's text, the instinct to leave the house and run on bare feet straight to the address Fahri had sent had overwhelmed him.

The streets were empty, and the sky, the color of lead, hung dark and low as he drove.

As usual Maryam's head had stayed cool. It was her idea to contact Imam Al-Bashir and have him set up the cover story, her idea for Recai to navigate to the address through the catacombs. But his body already knew the way.

He pulled up in front of the mosque and breathed deeply, pulling on what strength he had.

Recai's body ached to return to the caves, to act. Instead he forced himself to be still and find the strength Allah had given him. He was the one who ran, who acted without thinking. He was the man who screwed everything up, who let people down. He wasn't the man anyone should count on. He hadn't inherited that gene from his parents.

Now he was called to be more than that, and he felt unworthy. It had been easier when the situation landed in front of him. Without the time to consider the ramifications of his actions, he had defended Sabiha. Now he was intentionally involving himself in something purposeful. Was this even his business? Perhaps a coup was a good thing. The mayor was the worst thing ever to happen to the city.

Yet something about Fahri's text troubled him.

The ornate wooden door of the mosque opened, and an elderly Imam with a white beard appeared. His eyes peered into the darkness, searching for Recai's black car. When he found it, the emotion that flared in the old man's eyes made Recai's decision. It was hope that brought fire to the man's eyes.

Inside the mosque, Recai followed the man to the back rooms and down to the hidden caves beneath.

"Al-Bashir is a good man," the Imam spoke finally when the stairs reached the sand-packed floor of the softly lit tunnel.

"He is."

"He has faith in you. He believes that Allah has called on you."

"He does."

"Has he? Has Allah spoken to you?"

The Imam's eyes were bright, this time with excitement, as he asked.

"I don't know. I don't even know what I'm supposed to do."

"You're supposed to listen, to bend to the path that's been decided for you."

He spoke with the confidence of a person of faith. Recai was awed by a belief so deep there was no room for compromise. *Actions could be decided, people could be corrupted, but faith is the only thing left that could remain pure no matter what trials it endured.*

"A woman was here; she brought you this."

The Imam handed Recai a brown niqab, which was designed to cover a woman's face below her eyes. Recai smiled and hooked the sides over his ears, allowing his features to be hidden.

"Maryam?"

Nodding, the Imam smiled.

"She believes in you. Al-Bashir believes in you. Allah believes in you. And so do I."

"In'shallah," Recai replied before handing the Imam his keys and heading off into the caverns deep below the city, on his way to the address sent in the strange text message.

Isik waited until the room was full before nodding for the door to be shut. No one from outside was getting in now, and those in attendance were staying until he was ready to let them go.

Lighting another cigarette, he eyed the hidden office. Darya was in there, plotting his death he was sure. This betrayal would be the end of them. Isik loved her; she was his only sister, the only one who had known his father, the only one who knew just what he was capable of. She really shouldn't have been so surprised.

Isik stepped up onto the seat of a folding chair and watched as his presence commanded silence. This was power. To control without ever saying a word. He saw Darya's connections standing on the peripheries of the room, not wanting anyone to see them in association with this kind of underground movement. But the money was here, and their loyalty followed the cash.

"Brothers," Isik began with a low voice. The men unconsciously leaned in or stepped closer to hear him. *Power does not lie with the man who screams, but with the one who whispers.*

"My name is Dayar Yildirim. Some of you know me by other names. Some of you know my assistant, but you are all indebted to me. I have freed you. I have freed the city."

Isik paused, looking out, waiting for his words to register. The group was eclectic: men in suits, men in uniforms, men in taqiyahs of all colors. With a single breath they waited, united in anticipation of his next words.

"The mayor is gone. He will not be returning. It has been too long that he's stood apart from the daily lives of his people, so much so that I have been able to take his money and his power without him ever noticing. His final moments were pathetic, like a dog pleading for his life. He whimpered like a woman."

He sneered, inhaling the nicotine from his cigarette before tossing it aside. Smoke swirled in the room, and the temperature rose. Brought together in fear, the men faced Isik and the future he promised.

"With our leader so far from the reality of the streets, crime has sprung back up. Drugs have been infiltrating our homes, and women are allowed freedoms The Prophet never intended."

Heads nodded, encouraging him to continue. Isik stepped down from the chair, pulling the attention of the room as he moved. His voice rose as he continued, flowing in waves over the crowd, inciting even the withdrawn men to a call for change. All around him men from high above his social standing and those who worked every day for what little food they had came together in fear and the promise of something greater.

"The paper says our city is in decay, that we need a hero like The SandStorm to protect our women. But why? Why are these women out walking the streets alone at night at all? Because the mayor lost sight of his responsibility and became bloated with his own power and prestige. Without him, we have a choice. We can let our city fall farther into decay. Our women and children can wander unsupervised, and the vices of the West can continue to seep into our streets. Or, we can join together, take the reins of this driverless coach, and steer our people back to the right.

"We need curfews for our women!" Isik proclaimed.

"Yes!" a man in a suit cried out.

"We need respect for our officers!"

"Yes!"

"We need freedom from corruption and greed!"

"Yes!" The crowd cheered.

"We are leaderless. Who will lead you?"

"Dayar Yildirim!" a man in the back called.

"Dayar Yildirim!" another cried.

"Day-ar, Day-ar, Day-ar..." the chant began, rising in pitch as the men wrapped their arms around one another in celebration.

Isik watched as the frenzy of revolution rocked through the crowd. Alone these men were pawns; together they were his army. He smiled broadly, relishing the sound of his success, then wrapped an arm around a young man with curly hair who had been standing near the front of the crowd.

"Everything will change now, Brother. All our dreams will come true," Isik promised.

"Even mine," the strange man agreed, passion and determination in his voice.

From the tunnels below the city, Recai reached his destination and climbed out, entering the sewer system before going aboveground. Below ground he had navigated instinctively, unable to see through the darkness but sensing the movement and location of the sand that called him, drove him forward, whispered to him the secrets of the colonized desert. The alley was black now that night had fallen. His eyes were sharp, able to make out even the subtle changes of the wind by watching the sand that rode its current.

Recai spotted a fire escape and climbed the narrow metal rungs. Hand over hand he climbed easily, scaling the wall of the building until he reached a small window. He peered through from his perch two stories above the alley. Although there was only one dim lamp in the room, the smoke reflected its light, creating an ocean of fumes around the figures who had gathered.

At the back of the room there was a man standing on a chair, speaking animatedly. When he stepped down to address the crowd more intimately, he turned his head to the left, giving Recai a direct look at the snake eyes tattooed onto his skin.

Fury flashed through Recai. His skin tightened as his muscles involuntarily tensed. He was taken back in time to when Rebekah had lain across his lap, eyes wide as she was violated again and again. He remembered his uselessness as he lay injured, unable to do anything. Leaning forward, Recai carefully lifted the window so he could listen. Particles of sand drifted past him into the warehouse. The man's words were meaningless, making no promises, making no real statement, only provoking the fears and pandering to the egos of the gathered crowd.

When a chant began, Recai's mind reeled with sudden recognition: Dayar Yildirim was the Board Member who couldn't be found for questioning about the money missing from Osman Corps.

Recai waited until the crowd was in a frenzy before raising the window higher. He swung his legs through the opening and crept inside the warehouse, using exposed pipes and scaffolding to climb to the floor. Crouching low, he backed silently into the clothing racks before anyone could identify his presence.

No one looked his way; the crowd was too wrapped up in its own momentum. He moved through the racks, creeping forward toward Dayar Yildirim. A rapist, a Board Member, an RTK officer, a financier. The numbers didn't add up for Recai.

Recai slunk down an aisle left open between racks of clothing. The oppressive head of the badly ventilated warehouse bore down on him as sand shone in the air around him. Its presence surrounded him, further obscuring him in the dim light. Boxes of clothing were piled around him, some open, some stacked haphazardly. The chanting continued, rising into a fevered pitch, giving Recai the perfect opportunity to attack from behind.

Ducked low, he rushed out behind the tattooed man and pulled his arm back in a crippling lock. The curly-haired man who had been standing with Dayar fell to the ground and yelled out, even as the chanting crowd dropped into a hush.

"Let go of me!" Dayar seethed, pulling against his grip until Recai had no choice but to wrap a forearm around his neck. Recai held him tight, his muscular arm pushing into the rapist's jugular vein. The desire to squeeze until the man hung limply in his hold raged within Recai, making him pant as he restrained not just his enemy, but also his fury.

"Dayar!" the young man who had fallen yelled as he struggled to stand up.

Recai backed away from the crowd as they ceased their celebration and turned their full attention to the masked man. The smoke in the air became denser as sand began to rise in compliment to Recai's adrenalin.

"This man is not who you think," Recai proclaimed.

"It's The SandStorm!" someone cried out from the crowd.

"You cannot follow this insanity! This man is not a leader. He's a rapist and a murderer!" Recai continued.

"And what are you?" his captive hissed. "A coward behind a woman's veil, sneaking in the night—Allah only knows what you've been doing out there!"

Recai's fury rose in spite of his best efforts at self-control, and the air in the warehouse began to move. Sand and grit drifted through the room, slowly at first but picking up speed. The hanging garments moved with the wind, filling the open space with the whisper of fabric.

From deep within Recai another voice rose, and as he opened his mouth to speak, The Prophet's words were repeated: *Do you then feel secure that He will not cause a side of the land to swallow you up, or that He will not send against you a violent Sandstorm?*

The men nearest Recai hesitated at being reminded of their beliefs. With Recai's attention on the crowd his hold on

Dayar loosened, allowing the murderer enough leverage to slam his elbow up into Recai's ribs.

Recai called out and crushed Dayar in his arms. He growled before the mob rushed forward.

Dragging Dayar with him, Recai knocked over the shadeless floor lamp, shattering the bulb and dropping them all into darkness. The wind accelerated and every remaining speck of sand within the room rose into the air. Chaos consumed the crowd as some ran blind for the only door and others searched for their new leader.

Weaving through the racks, Recai dragged Dayar until the man dug in his heels and brought them both to a stop.

"I go nowhere with you!" he screamed and finally wrenched out of Recai's hold. Over his shoulder, Recai could see smoke rising from where the lamp had been. The exposed wires or one of the many discarded cigarettes had ignited the clothing.

"We have to leave, now!" Recai reached out to grab Dayar, but the man had pulled something out of his pocket and was backing away.

"The whole place is going to burn! You aren't safe!"

"You are so right about that," Dayar sneered before lunging, aiming the tip of his butterfly knife toward Recai's throat.

Recai watched the knife move through the air. He lifted his arm in defense, turning as he ducked. The knife slid deep into his shoulder.

Recai sunk to his knees in pain and yanked the knife out, dropping it to the ground. The blade had missed his artery but cut deep into the muscle. Blood oozed from his wound. The screams of the murderous crowd shifted from lust for blood to fear for their lives as the fire blazed across the racks, surrounding them in flames. Dayar had fled.

The wind stopped. Sand hovered in the air for a moment before falling to the ground around Recai.

He knelt within a circle of sand which grew until his entire body was covered with a light dusting.

"There you are!" a familiar voice said, reaching out for him. Looking up Recai saw the terrified face of Fahri Kana. "We have to get you out of here. There's no way you aren't going to get the blame for this insanity."

"I know. I couldn't stop him."

"If it wasn't him, there would just be someone else. Let's go!"

Fire rushed forward, wrapping around the two men until they were surrounded by the hungry flames. With a grunt Recai pulled himself up, refusing Fahri's help.

"I can't go out through the front," Recai said.

"In the back, there's access to the alley. All these buildings have one."

He began to run toward the rear of the building, but Recai heard a scream from the main door that stopped him in his tracks.

"Kana!" he called and ran in the other direction.

Rushing through the flames, Recai choked on the black smoke. The chemicals used to dye the clothing were being released with the heat and flames, poisoning the air until it was toxic. His shoulder throbbed, and his left arm screamed in pain as he moved toward the sound of the voice.

"Where the hell are you going?" Fahri called out, catching up to him.

"There's someone up there!"

"I'll get him and go out the front. You get out!"

Recai turned and ran while Fahri pulled a man with wild, curly hair out from beneath a fallen supply shelf.

In the back of the warehouse, Recai searched for a gate or a door that led to the alley. Smoke and fire tore through the building, consuming the walls and storage boxes stacked tall. Behind one of the shelves Recai heard another call.

"Help me! I'm..." the voice coughed, choking on the toxins in the air.

"Where are you?" Recai yelled.

196

"Here!" Another cough. Recai followed the hacking to identify the voice's origin. Around the corner, surrounded by ash and smoke, sat the man Recai had set out to capture. He was sitting on the ground, blood pouring from a wound over his eyes. Smashed pallets lay on the ground around him.

"Help me." The man looked up into Recai's eyes. "They fell on me. I think my leg's broken!"

Recai stared at him before turning away.

"No . . ." Recai's voice was low, barely audible above the crackling flames closing in around them.

"Please!"

He stopped. Fire crackled around him, nearly reaching the tall ceiling now.

"Who are you?"

"Dayar Yildirim."

"No. You're a thug, a rapist."

Recai turned and spat, stepping closer, feeling his strength return. Lust for justice pounded through his veins. The fire blazed hotter, and voices could be heard in the distance over the din of destruction.

"No…" the man protested.

"You are nothing! All you are is the shit that burns in the desert sun, and you can burn here."

"My name is Isik," the man confessed.

"Nice to meet you, Isik. Tell the angel Malik I said hello."

Recai turned and strode toward the back wall to search for the alley exit. He heard the man's sobs over the crackling fire, but ignored them. Against the wall he found an old door which opened easily. Stepping through the doorway he found a gate which separated the warehouse from the alley. It was rusty and old and looked as if it hadn't been used in years. He pulled against it, trying to force it open. Pain ripped through his shoulder as he did, but it finally moved.

Outside there was a small alley, which led out to the main road in front of the warehouse. Sirens blared as the RTK and fire brigade arrived.

Taking a deep breath of the smoke-free air outside, Recai paused, then turned and ran back in to the flames.

Isik had passed out leaning against a smoking wall. Soon the entire room would be too hot to attempt a rescue, and anyone inside would be lost. Recai leaned down and lifted the man upright. His shoulder roared as the injured muscle tore itself farther apart.

Each step was labored. Recai's left arm refused to continue, and hung limp at his side. With one arm he pulled Isik—the rapist, the murderer—out of the fire. Dragging his body against the concrete floor, Recai didn't worry about any injuries the man might incur. He'd be alive; that was more than Rebekah got and more than they'd meant for him. But Allah had sent him here. He couldn't leave another man to die.

Outside, Recai dropped Isik. The man would live. Someone would find him, and if not, he'd recover. Pain swirled in Recai's mind, threatening to overtake his conscious thoughts. With his left arm still hanging limp, Recai approached a manhole cover. From here he could find his way back down to the tunnels.

Kneeling next to the iron cover Recai despaired. One hand was not enough to move it off. Silently he prayed.

As he knelt, the sand on the street and in the air swirled together. Soon a wind picked up, and Recai opened his eyes to see a small tornado gaining momentum and force. The funnel did not move about, only hovered before him. Reaching out, Recai allowed his hand to be surrounded by the force. He could feel the velocity, but it did not rip through him the way it seemed it should.

"Lift," he whispered, praying to Allah to save him, if it be his will.

The small tornado grew larger, spinning furiously. Recai removed his hand and stood up, pulling away from the tornado.

198

He watched as it touched down on the manhole cover and lifted it into the air, where it hovered next to Recai. He climbed in and down the ladder, using one hand to keep his balance, the other braced against his side.

When he reached the bottom, the cover dropped from the sky back into place. Sand from the tornado drifted through the holes and landed silently at his feet.

Recai knelt down on the grated ground above the water and laid his head before him. Prostrate to God he swore, whatever was happening to him, he would use it in the name of Allah. He would redeem himself and his people. He would be a SandStorm of redemption.

EPILOGUE

Each shift in the air, each movement, ran along her flesh like a tidal wave of pain. She sat letting the flood wash over her—drowning her in a sea of unbelievable consequences. Inside and out her nerves were raw, screaming against the onslaught of sensations.

Months had passed since the fire. Her burns healed, leaving her scabbed and oozing. The dark room surrounded her, its curtains drawn, keeping out the curious glances of the stars. None had ever seen anything as hideous as this woman.

Her beauty flaked away as the healing flesh reformed. Deep, puckered scars formed where delicate skin had once been, running along the length of a body that would never be seen by a man again. New skin, purple and tender grew across her scalp and down her back. Its thickness ensured her hair would not return.

Meals were left outside her door as she sat, tearless agony pulsing through her body. Together with her pain, anger held her close, feeding her will to survive. Yearning for freedom, she had reached and failed. Allah was twisted. The story was the same in every lie, and her disappointment animated her features until the only recognizable part of her were her eyes. Even those were distant and driven.

She sat with nothing better to do than replay her betrayal and pain. What had she become? A monster in the memory of a woman. The person she used to be never considered failure, and now, mutilated and shattered, she drowned in hatred.

He had come to see her. Her brother. Her enemy. Her friend.

He would come again, forcing himself to look at her destroyed beauty. She did not try to conceal it from him, sitting naked and raw. Without clothing her pain was dulled, only the air stung as she moved. She had been without clothing her entire stay at the private medical center where she was treated, as well as during her convalescence at home.

Standing slowly she walked to the bed, agony clenching down as she looked at the black garment lying there, mocking her. She had longed for freedom. Dreamed of a world where she could be herself no matter where she was, where she could command the power and respect she deserved. She spent her entire life clawing out of the hole of oppression her uncle had buried her in.

She pulled the loose dress over her head, which fell down to her feet, covering the white and purple splotches that riddled her brown legs. Slipping her feet into the black slippers in front of her, she pushed her arms into the sleeves of the shapeless gown. Leaving the hood hanging down her back, she reached down for the black gloves she had requested.

Her nails were gone, replaced by scar tissue. Despite the ripping of scabs along her fingers, she pulled the tight gloves on until they reached her elbow, high above the bottom of her sleeves.

Looking in the mirror, she saw how her upper lip had melted away and her nose no longer had a distinct shape on the left side. What little hair remained were mere wisps compared to her former locks, thick and beautiful. She covered her head with a skull cap—black, like the rest of her garb.

The hood fit snugly over her head, wrapping around her neck and flowing into her dress easily, creating a perfect picture of piety. Pulling her disfigured lips up into a smile, she placed the niqab over her nose and hooked it to her ears, covering the rest of her face so only her eyes remained visible.

Now she was nothing. She disappeared into the blackness of her rooms, dissipating into the air like smoke. All that remained was a shadow on the wall.

A READER'S COMPANION TO:

SHADOW
ON THE WALL

Interview with

PAVARTI K TYLER

Q : *Shadow on the Wall* is a very ambitious work. With what parts of the writing process did you struggle?

A: *Shadow* flowed very naturally for me. The relationships and characters made sense from the very beginning. However, the subject matter I wanted to tackle is tricky. I was advised by a number of people to write a different story or write it a different way. But to shy away from the authenticity of my characters just because it was uncomfortable seemed dishonest. I owed them more than that. So the process of staying true to the story I needed to tell despite a publishing and cultural climate which was constantly telling me to sanitize it was extremely difficult.

Q: What inspired you to write such a heavy story?

A: I certainly hope those who read *Shadow on the Wall* will enjoy the story, but I wrote this story not only to entertain but to inspire examination of the world around us. Our civilization is at a breaking point. People are taking sides and oppression is closing in on all of us. From religion to politics to the general cultural climate it seems everyone is on high alert. In my experience though, people – average, everyday people – are not so different from each other. Perhaps writing such a dark story is my call to action; this is the nightmare waiting for us at the end of the tunnel. What will it take for each of us to stand up for what we believe in? Recai has a calling, a mission. He is given his path. We are not. When faced with a choice between oppression and freedom, between standing up for someone else or sitting back and watching the sky fall, what will you do? Will you choose to live like Maryam, seeing the good in people and finding a way to make the world better? I hope so.

Q: What was the research process like for this novel?

A: The research for *Shadow* was intense. I've done this kind of research for other authors and playwrights before but never for myself. The process of taking that research and reorganizing it internally so the details of a culture can be conveyed without sounding like a lecture was the most difficult part. Since I'm neither Turkish, Kurdish nor Muslim there were a lot of small details requiring research. I have studied religion extensively and being a bit of a superhero aficionado that aspect of the book was less of a challenge. My training as a dramaturge prepared me for this kind of research but nothing compares to the experience of so completely stepping outside of myself into the shoes of not only another person but another culture.

Q: Why did you choose to set *Shadow on the Wall* in Turkey?

A: Elih, Turkey is a real place, although it is nothing like the fictional city I created. When I set out to write a story set in the Middle East, I looked at maps and wanted somewhere ripe with history and culture but not in the current crosshairs. Turkey is positioned between Europe and the Middle East, populated by Muslims, Jews and Christians and has a historical conflict between the Turks, Arabs and Kurds living there. It was the ideal location.

While *Shadow* touches on issues relevant in the world today, I didn't want to write another post 9-11 story about the Taliban or al-Qaeda. Turkey was a good solution because it is rich in culture, plus Elih is the Kurdish name for the real city of Batman, Turkey. And when writing a superhero story, how could I resist setting it in Batman!

Q: Did your own religious views or upbringing contribute to your choice of religions featured in this novel? Why didn't Christianity make the list?

A: My religious views most definitely played a part in my choice to write this story. As a Unitarian Universalist I believe that each person has the right to find their own path to God. While we embrace all religions the first tenant of UUism is that we affirm and promote the inherent worth and dignity of every person. When I look around me and see the increasing number of hate crimes, women forced to both cover and uncover against their will, the fear mongering and profiling that occurs in the political arena internationally and the general rise of Islamaphobia, my own beliefs demanded that I say something.

Christianity only played a periphery role in *Shadow on the Wall* as it wasn't appropriate in the plot to include at this point. However, in *Prisoners of the Wind*, book 2 of *The SandStorm Chronicles*, Christianity will play a more prevalent role.

Q: Which character do you relate to most? Which character was hardest to write?

A: Of all the characters I'm most drawn to Darya. Her story is so tragic but I can see how the circumstances of her life took her down that path. I imagine being in her circumstance and I get frustrated for her; to be so smart and capable, to have such ambition and no way to express it, plus the privilege she has adds an extra layer of confinement. I don't mean to imply this is the case for all women in Muslim countries. Maryam is an example of that! However, were I Darya, I think it would be easy to become angry and bitter. Taken to the extreme I can even see how that could drive a person a little insane.

As for the most difficult, Recai took me a long time to wrap my brain around. Other characters shone brightly in my mind, leading me through their stories and teaching me about themselves. Recai, however, much like in the book, was more elusive. Because he doesn't have a clear sense of himself or who he wants to be, it was difficult to convey him as a three dimensional character instead of just a big whiner. Thanks to some amazing advice from friends and my brilliant editor, I think he has come into his own, and by the end of the book we all have a clearer understanding of who he is.

Q: There is a strong focus on women's issues in *Shadow*. Would you consider this a feminist book?

A: No. I'm not interested in telling the story of one gender over the other. I think the situation for women in *Shadow* is as much of a concern and issue for the men. As with any conflict, there are two sides. Darya is a woman who despises women for their weakness. If anything she's the biggest misogynist of the entire book. This isn't a book about men and women; that is a vehicle through which we explore ideas of power and corruption.

Q: There are some similarities to Batman in Recai's character. Was this on purpose? Did you include traits from any other superheroes in the novel?

A: Certainly *Shadow on the Wall* is reminiscent of the Batman mythos. The Bruce Wayne/Batman dichotomy is my favorite superhero story. While Recai doesn't have the same back story as Bruce Wayne, the creation of his character did happen as an homage to Batman. The archetype of the anti-hero or the resistant savior is extremely appealing to me as a storyteller. Recai's internal conflict and inability to reconcile his own insecurities and doubt with the demands of his faith pulled me in and kept his story going far past the limits of Batman

Q: Why did you choose to describe violent scenes in vivid details rather than simply letting it remain implied? Are you concerned you will lose any of your potential audience because of the graphic nature of some of the scenes?

A: We do not live in a bubble. Life is messy and painful and full of awful things. In the beginning of the story Recai really has no concept of this. His experience of Rebekah's rape and murder is cataclysmic. In order for us to follow along with his evolution and struggle we have to see what he sees and feel what he feels. If that feeling was revulsion, anger, pain, outrage, so be it. The reader must feel it too. It is certainly possible that some readers will turn away from this. I understand that. However, the evil of the oppression is in many ways an additional character who cannot be sanitized or avoided. In order to truly understand the evolution of Recai, Darya, Maryam, Isik, Hasad, Fahri, Sabiha and Abdullah, you must understand how deeply demented their world has become.

Q: What type of reader will most enjoy *Shadow on the Wall*? What type would most benefit from reading it?

A: This is a novel written for adults. It is not intended for children or teenagers; both thematically and because of the explicit content. However, there is a universal appeal to the characters. As much as you may dislike Isik and Darya, they are relatable. Their circumstances are untenable and at a certain pressure point all of us will break. The question is will you heed the call of the desert or burn?

Q: There are so many life lessons woven into the novel, what do you hope people will gain from reading *Shadow on the Wall*?

A: My hope is that people will read *Shadow* and see that we are not so different. No matter what culture, what religion, what gender we may be, the reality is: life is hard. We all need a hero and we all need someone who will believe in us even when we don't believe in ourselves. So the next time you see a woman in the grocery store with a scarf on her head, don't ignore her, don't look away, instead smile and say hello. She may have something to teach you.

DISCUSSION GUIDE

1. *Shadow on the Wall* uses of both the magical and the mundane to create a world in which a modern day superhero is plausible. How does the author bring these factors together to create a believable creation story? How would life have been different for Recai had Rebekah not been killed?

2. Each section of the novel is introduced with a religious quote, or epigraph. What was the purpose of these and how did they relate to the corresponding sections?

3. Describe Recai's emotions during the attack on Rebekah. What is the source of Recai's declaration to marry her, despite their religious differences? What impact does her death have on his development as a hero?

4. The struggles of the women of Elih are representative of the larger inequalities of women throughout the world. What is the purpose of placing this story within the Muslim culture? How does gender play a role in the current political climate within the Middle East?

5. What events in the story support Maryam's observation that "man [is] perhaps a worse threat to humanity's soul than any devil"? Do you agree with this statement? Explain.

6. What was your first impression of Darya? What does her refusal to fit into a niche say about the kind of person she

is? How did your understanding of her character change as the story evolved?

7. "The RTK were charged with upholding the moral law of Islam, but more often than not, they were the very ones breaking that code." Give some real life examples of situations where those charged with upholding the law were also the ones to corrupt it.

8. Darya and Maryam have different feelings about the hijab: one views the headscarf as freeing, the other as confining. How would you feel in their situations? Do you think hijab is a protective or oppressive measure? Does your opinion change when discussing niqab or the burqa? Does it make a difference if wearing one is the woman's choice?

9. Images of the landscape and sand recur throughout *Shadow on the Wall*. Discuss passages where the sand appears and consider its symbolism. When is the sand destructive? When is it not?

10. What makes Isik such a compelling antagonist? Discuss what it is about him that appeals to you as a reader? What does his relationship with Darya reveal about him? How does his story resemble Recai's and how does it differ?

11. Through your reading of *Shadow on the Wall,* what were you particularly surprised by? Explain how this book might help to challenge prejudice about Islam and the variety of people who follow Muhammad. What assumptions did you bring to the book? Have they changed?

12. How do the men in the story react to the violence against women? How are they different? How are they the same? In what ways does religion inform their reactions, if at all?

13. Consider the author's unflinching depictions of violence and gender inequality alongside the work of other writers. How does *Shadow on the Wall* compare to similar themes presented in such disparate works as Margaret Atwood's *Handmaid's Tale,* Laleh Khadivi's *Age of Orphans,* Neil Gaiman's *American Gods,* and Salman Rushdie's *Satanic Verses?*

14. Although Tyler's novel illuminates one very specific time and place, her depictions of cultural confinement and corruption can be applied to many other settings. In what ways do you identify personally with the themes and issues in *Shadow on the Wall?*

15. Discuss the author's unique writing style and refer to passages that are particularly poetic or moving. What does the use of multiple voices contribute to the novel? How would the story be different if it were narrated only through Recai's eyes?

GLOSSARY

- Bey – Turkish prefix for men as in Mr.
- Beyan – Turkish prefix for women as in Mrs.
- Burqa – A burqa is an enveloping outer garment worn by women in some Islamic traditions to cover their bodies in public places. This is often considered one garment which covers hair, bust and eyes.
- But those who wronged among them changed the words to a statement other than that which had been said to them. So we sent upon them a punishment from the sky for the wrong that they were doing. (Surah 7:162, Qu'ran)
- Djinn – An invisible spirit mentioned in the Qu'ran and believed by Muslims to inhabit the earth and influence mankind by appearing in the form of humans or animals. Often correlated to demons or genies in Western mythology.
- Do you then feel secure that He will not cause a side of the land to swallow you up, or that He will not send against you a violent Sandstorm? (Surah 17:68, Qu'ran)
- Effendi – Turkish title given to a man of high social standing or education.
- Egirdir Commando – Fictitious unit of the Turkey Military based on the intense training provident soldiers in the Egirdir Mountain Commando School and Education Center.

217

- Fatimah – Muhammad's daughter with first wife Khadijah. Wife of Ali and mother of Hasan and Husain. Fatimah is regarded as a loving and devoted daughter, mother, wife, a sincere Muslim, and an exemplar for women. She is reported to have been the confidant and an advisor of her father and husband.
- Fistic – Term of endearment, literally "peanut"
- Golems – From Jewish folklore, an animated anthropomorphic being, created entirely from inanimate matter.
- Got veren – Turkish insult loosely translated to "ass giver."
- Hajj – Pilgrimage to Mecca, Saudi Arabia. It is one of the largest pilgrimages in the world, and is the fifth pillar of Islam, a religious duty that must be carried out at least once in their lifetime by every able-bodied Muslim who can afford to do so.
- Halal – Arabic word meaning lawful or permitted. The term is used to designate any object or action which is permissible to use or engage in, according to Islamic law. The term is used to designate food seen as permissible.
- Hasankeyf – An ancient town and district located along the Tigris River in the Batman Province in southeastern Turkey. Hasankeyf's origin as a settlement area probably dates back to prehistoric times. The city was the pivot of Turkish culture with its plentiful educational and scientific institutes. It was declared a natural conservation area by Turkey in 1981.
- Hijab – Refers to both the head covering traditionally worn by Muslim women and modest Muslim styles of dress in general. The Arabic word translates to "curtain" or "cover." Most Islamic legal systems define this type of modest dressing as covering everything except the face and hands in public. Many divergent views exist about the necessity and definition of hijab.

- In'shallah – Arabic translates to "God willing"
- Inna lillahi wa inna ilahi raji'un – Translates to" "Who, when a misfortune overtakes them, say: 'Surely we belong to Allah and to Him shall we return.'" (Surah 2:156, Qu'ran) This is the phrase that Muslims recite when a person suffers some kind of loss and is usually recited upon hearing the news of someone's death.
- Isha prayer – Last of the five prayer times in a day. This can be performed anytime before dawn the next day but is ideally done before half the night is over.
- Israelite Asiyah – Asiyah was the Israelite wife of the Pharaoh who discovered Moses in the river. Asiyah is said to have worshiped God in secret and praying in disguise fearing her husband. She died while being tortured by her husband, who had discovered her monotheism. According to Hadith, she will be among the first women to enter Paradise because she accepted Moses' monotheism over the Pharaoh's beliefs.
- Jahannam – One of the many names for Hell in Islam. Jahannam refers specifically to the depth of its pit. Descriptions of hell are detailed and full of torture.
- Kahretsin – Turkish for "damn."
- Karakucak – A Turkish folk wrestling style practiced nationwide and sanctioned by the Turkish Wrestling Federation.
- Kum firtinasi – Turkish for "Sandstorm," a strong wind carrying sand particles through the air. They are low level occurrences, usually only ten feet in height not more than fifty feet above the surface. Due to the frequent winds created by surface heating, they are most predominate during the day and die out in the night.
- Laa ela-ha el-lal-la – Arabic for "There is no god but Allah."

- Malik - Malik is known as the angel of hell to Muslims, who recognize Malik as an archangel. Malik is in charge of maintaining Jahannam (hell) and carrying out God's command to punish the people in hell.
- Marussia B2 – Second in a series of coupes built by Marussia Motors. Sporty, high-tech, and elegant, the Marussia B-2 comes with three flat panel touch displays, 420 horsepower, and tops out at over 160mph.
- Masha'Allah – Translates to "as God has willed." This phrase is used when admiring or praising something or someone, in recognition that all good things come from God and are blessings from Him.
- Mecca – Mecca was the birth place of Muhammad and is the most sacred place in Islam. The Ka'ba is a mosque (built by Abraham, according to Muslim tradition) is in Mecca, Saudi Arabia, built around a black stone. The Prophet Muhammad designated Mecca as the holy city of Islam and the direction (qibla) in which all Muslims should offer their prayers.
- Muezzin – A man appointed to call to prayer climbs the mineret of the mosque, and he calls in all directions, "Hasten to prayer." The professional muezzin is chosen for his good character, voice and skills to serve at the mosque; he, however, is not considered a cleric.
- Muslimah – A Muslim woman.
- Niqab – A piece of cloth which covers the face below the eyes worn by some Muslim women as a part of their modest dress.
- Nogai tea – A Turkish drink prepared by boiling milk and tea together with butter, salt and pepper.
- Only an honorable man treats women with honor and integrity. And only a mean, deceitful, and dishonest man humiliates and insults women. (This Hadith is reported by Ibn 'Asaker)

- Purdah – System of sex segregation, practiced especially by keeping women in seclusion. In some Muslim communities women who are unmarried but have begun puberty are kept in strict seclusion to maintain their purity.
- Qu'ran – Holy Book of Islam is considered the direct word of God as recited by the Prophet Muhammad. The Qu'ran is divided into 114 surahs (sections or chapters of unequal length).
- Quibla – The direction of Mecca from any point in the world.
- Rak'ah – Movements and words recited during prayer.
- Roma – Ethnic group with origins in Northern India and Romania. Widely referred to as Gypsies.
- Sajdah – Prostration to Allah. The position involves having the forehead, nose, both hands, knees, and all toes touching the ground together.
- Salaam alaikum – Islamic greeting meaning "peace be upon you"
- Saqar – One of the names of Hell (Jahannam) mentioned in the Qu'ran.
- Shalom – Hebrew word meaning peace, completeness, and welfare and can be used to mean both hello and goodbye.
- Shariah law – Islamic Moral Code and Religious Law based on the Qu'ran and example of the Prophet Muhammad's life. Modernists, traditionalists, and fundamentalists all hold different views of sharia, as do adherents to different schools of Islamic thought and scholarship. Different countries, societies and cultures have varying interpretations of sharia as well.
- Shik turban – A garment worn by a man in the Shik religion in keeping with the five articles of faith. The turban is intended as protection for the Tenth Gate or spiritual opening at the top of the head.

- Siktir lan – Translates to "fuck off."
- Taqiyahs – a short, rounded cap worn by some observant Muslim men to emulate the Prophet Muhammad and his companions, who were never seen without their heads covered.
- The Prophet tells us "Let not compassion move you in their case." (Surah 24:2, Qu'ran)
- Ulama - The educated class of Muslim legal scholars engaged in the several fields of Islamic studies. They are best known as the arbiters of shariah law, but the term is also used to describe the body of Muslim clergy who have completed several years of training and study of Islamic sciences.
- Ululation – A long, wavering, high-pitched lament.
- Ummah – Arabic word for community or nation. Often used to describe the entire Muslim world.
- Walaikum as salaam - The standard response to "salaam alaikum" meaning "And upon you be peace."
- We sent upon them a punishment from the sky for the wrong that they were doing. (Surah 7:160, Qu'ran)
- Zina – Islamic sin of unlawful sexual intercourse, primarily adultery, fornication, having sexual intercourse without being married.

ABOUT THE AUTHOR

Pavarti K Tyler is an artist, wife, mother and number cruncher. She graduated Smith College in 1999 with a degree in Theatre. After graduation, she moved to New York, where she worked as a Dramaturge, Assistant Director and Production Manager on productions both on and off Broadway.

Later, Pavarti went to work in the finance industry as a freelance accountant for several international law firms. She now operates her own accounting firm in the Washington DC area, where she lives with her husband, two daughters and two terrible dogs. When not preparing taxes, she is busy penning her next novel.

Throughout history, literature and the art of story-telling have influenced politics, religion and culture. The power of the epic tale is universal. Why is it that those who never read The Iliad know Helen of Troy? Her story, Homer's story, transcends the written word and has become a part of our human lexicon. The power of the written word is undeniable and Pavarti is honored to be part of the next wave of literary revolution.

You can follow her on Facebook, Twitter or her blog.

www.fightingmonkeypress.com

two moons
of
Sera

Prologue

Nilafay ran, slipping on the unfamiliar terrain, desperate to reach water. The rocks dug into the thin flesh of her webbed feet, cutting her skin. This place was so foreign despite being only miles from her home. Never had she seen the sun so bright or felt the moisture evaporate directly off her skin; she was sure she would die from the cruelty of the atmosphere.

It was difficult to navigate her way through the wilderness, but now she breathed in the familiar briny scent of home. She licked her lips, seeking relief from the dryness before stepping out of the tree line and onto the rocky beach. The sun overwhelmed her sensitive eyes. She slid thin, clear membranes over her eyes. She had always considered them vestigial, before coming above water to the Erdland.

She moved forward, wincing as the heat of the sun burned her delicate forehead. Her irises retracted and for a moment she was blinded, but she could smell and taste the salt in the air, leading her to the water. The rest of Nilafay's senses were on high alert, her eardrums straining to feel the vibrations of distant voices.

Frantic to reach the surf, she slipped and ripped open her shin. She bit down on her lip, refusing to cry out or shed a tear. She was done crying. Nilafay heard them calling from further back in the forest; the hunters who had seduced her with offers of friendship and a world unlike any she had seen before. They were closing in, the creatures they commanded following her scent, leading their masters closer. She shivered at the memory of their strange hair covered bodies. At first she had been intrigued by the animals with the eyes of men, but when she learned that they were there not to befriend her but to guard and cage her she resented their tracking gaze.

Nilafay stood and resumed her pitch toward the coast line, pressing through the throbbing in her leg. The sensitive myomere muscles of her body were unaccustomed to impact injury. The hunters approached the tree line noisily, making no attempt to hide their arrival. She dropped to her knees. Her iridescent white flesh shone in the morning sun, its lack of pigment reflecting the bright light beating down on her. The rocky beach offered no asylum.

The men grew louder, closer with each passing moment, speaking their gruff language. She understood only a few words. But what she did understand terrified her: "net, experiment, animal, project, cage..."

Please, just let me get to the water...

16 Years Later

The sand softened my impact when I landed; jumping from the tree I'd used to climb over the rock wall separating my home from the outside world. I released a shaky breath. I'd ventured further out into the forest today, further than I would have if my mother had been around. Without her here I didn't bother sneaking back in like usual. I'd spent the day exploring as much as I wanted, and I longed to know about everything outside the small cove I lived in.

I'd never been beyond the mountain range overshadowing our home; only through the forest leading south toward the villages. The danger of discovery, or worse, capture, kept me from going too far. I didn't know what would happen if the Erdlanders found us. My mother's stories about needles and tests and tortures from before I was born were enough to keep me on a tight leash.

The water beyond the cove led north, into the ocean; where the Sualwet people lived. My mother's people. We were refugees from that world, too. They exiled her, because of me.

My world held me tightly, like too-small clothing which refused to adjust as you grew. I was stifled and frustrated and lately I found I wanted to venture further, risking capture if only for a glimpse of an Erdlander. Mother said they had hair on their heads like me and some even had it on their faces. They walked like us and spoke words as we did, although the language was different. They didn't have gills and didn't absorb oxygen through their skin and they used their mouths to breathe. I wasn't like them and I wasn't like my mother's people. I was an anomaly, an accident of science, not supposed to exist. But my mother's escape from her prison before my birth meant I was here, alone on the shore.

"Serafay!" My mother called emerging from the water in time to see me walk out from the tree line. Her frown gave away her displeasure but she'd returned from scavenging with treasures to show me.

"Mother!" I waved my hand before reaching behind me and pulling my long chestnut hair into a knot.

"Always playing with that hair."

"Just because you don't have any doesn't mean you should be so jealous." I teased.

She laughed.

I splashed into the water so I could help carry the bags she dragged behind her.

"These were a lot lighter underwater."

"Give me one." I offered, holding out my hand to take some of her burden.

"No, you'll cheat and look." Her mock scowl was playful as she pretended to hold the bags protectively from me.

"Fine then, carry them yourself!" I dove under the surface and kicked off, letting the thin webbing between my toes capture the water and propel me forward.

I loved being underwater, the weightlessness of it surrounded and held me. The shallow cove was wide and I could swim out quite far before the ocean floor dropped off and I was in open sea. The call of the expanse was hard to deny but I couldn't go out today. It made my mother worry, like everything else, and I was anxious to see what she had brought home.

I could stay underwater for hours, as long as there was oxygen in one form or another, and I longed to lose myself in the sea. Eventually, I needed to resurface and use my lungs but the time I stole in the darkness of submersion soothed my dry skin and my lonely heart. Breaking the surface, a thin membrane, a gift from my mother's genetics, closed over my eyes protecting them from the sun's intense light. I paddled back to the shore in time to help her heave the bags up to the rock and cloth enclosure we called home.

The fire in our makeshift hearth had died, so I used the fire stone we'd salvaged in another treasure hunt to light a spark. I tried to be patient while Mother pulled a loose shift over her head, the thin cloth hanging down to her knees. We found or made most of our clothing, in keeping with the loose-fitting Erdlander style. Underwater people wore very little and what they did wear was always tight. It looked so uncomfortable to me. Mother said it helped her swim faster. I always swam naked because the fabric of clothes impeded my movement.

The makeshift home we'd built on the cove was comfortable. We had the supplies we needed and hammocks hanging between the sparse trees to sleep in. Recently, I had even separated the space into rooms, using the taut-weighted cloth the

Sualwet used as walls underwater. Mother had scavenged it from an abandoned home. Further back, a small cave in the rocky incline offered us shelter when we needed it, but we both preferred to stay outside.

A smile brightened her face as she approached where I sat next to the fire. "There was another attack." She sat on one of the woven chairs we'd made and began pulling something out of the bag. "The war seems to have gotten worse; there were a lot of bodies. It must have just happened and the sharks kept the other Sualwet away."

"Sharks!" I leaned toward her, terrified and excited by her adventure.

"Yes! Big ones, too. The water was red with gore."

"You shouldn't have gone near them!" My scolding tone was betrayed by my smile, I longed for anything half as exciting as what my mother described.

"They weren't interested in me, too busy gorging themselves on Erdlander blubber!" She laughed again. In her eyes, the misfortune of others paled to the misery of her life, it was hard for her to find sympathy. Some might call her cruel, but she was gentle under her hardened exterior.

"Besides, if those beasts hadn't died, this would've never been there for me to find." Out of the sack she pulled what appeared to be a butterfly made entirely out of stars. I reached forward; wanting to touch the sparkling thing to make sure it was real.

"It's a hair piece. They use it to decorate themselves." Taking the object in my hand, I was surprised by how its sturdy weight made it feel trustworthy. The other side was a simple metal mechanism which opened and shut on a lever. Not much different from the animal traps I made.

"It's amazing," My voice was just a whisper. I turned the gift over and over again before running my fingers lightly along the sparkling decoration.

"Let's put it in." Mother didn't usually like to touch my hair; she said it irritated her skin. Tonight, she jumped up and walked to the baskets I kept my personal things in and grabbed my small comb.

"When you were born, there was no hair on you anywhere, just as it should be." She began with a chuckle pulling the comb through my long locks. "And you were pink. Nothing like the other hatchlings I'd seen."

Evening settled around us and sun peaked from behind the ragged mountain top in the distance.

"But then, you weren't a hatchling were you?"

"No," I smiled, relaxing into her memory. It was nice to feel loved.

She laid the comb down and began running her fingers through my hair. It was an unusual moment of intimacy.

"Mom..."

"You scared everyone else, but I knew... I could see in your silver eyes that you were something worth protecting." She pulled my hair back from my temples and fumbled with the strange hair piece for a moment before it clasped with a click.

"Beautiful," she declared.

"Thank you." Looking behind me, I saw the wistful expression I had grown up with on her face. We had moments of happiness here in our little oasis, but my mother existed with a shroud of sorrow covering everything she did. Being away from her people was painful and I hated being the reason for it. "What else did you find?"

Dismissing her musings with a shake of her head, my mother came back around and reached into her bag.

One after the next, she pulled out treasures and necessities. She had recovered paper for me to dry in the sun, jars full of sea water (and one with a crab!). There were cooking utensils, ropes, clothes and even music on melodisks.

I sorted her loot into piles of things needing to be dried, repaired or cleaned while she inserted one of the new melodisks. The tonifier was old, but its power cells still worked.

Music rose from the box, low and vibrating, thrumming against me with its slow beat. Mother stepped back from the sound as if it somehow offended her, but didn't reach for the eject key. The music was like nothing I'd heard before. It was neither danceable, nor sing-able. I could make out no words and when voices finally joined the cacophony I was overcome with the need to move.

Taking her hand I pulled my mother out of the small enclosure and under the evening sky. The two moons above us shone in the dim light, one slightly larger and further away than the other. They gazed down upon us as our bodies took in the visceral intonations moving us.

In the corner of my eye I saw something flicker, as if the fire had somehow followed us and sparked in the night air. When I turned to look, it was gone.

Available Now on Amazon.com

DEVOUR

Amina Foxx
Stage 3
CDC Alerted – Awaiting Pickup
KGR-13 ND#7431

Amina moaned as she woke. The pain in her back had receded to a dull ache, but the glaring light seared through to her brain whether her eyes were open or closed.

She couldn't remember how long she'd been here; even her name eluded her. The pain, which had been her constant companion for so many weeks, blurred out all rational thought. Instead of thinking about her job and the days of work she had missed, she spent moment to moment in a quest to alleviate her agony.

White-blue light greeted her as she awoke, blinding her and making her lift an arm over her face.

The motion distracted her from the ice pick of light boring into her brain and brought her attention to the convulsion lashing through her shoulder. A scream ripped from her dry lips, an alien sound consisting of a gurgling, guttural voice Amina did not recognize as her own.

Muscles screamed as she pulled her aching body up into a sitting position, each movement ripping through her muscles and nerves. As the sheet fell away from her body, she felt as if something was peeling her skin away in slow, methodical movements. Sandpaper scraped against every surface of her skin. After an agonizing show of endurance, Amina rested back against her pillows, eyes still closed.

Falling back into what she had prayed would be a more comfortable position, Amina moaned. The desired relief that inspired the movement did not appear. The cool air chilled her; the delicate skin on her arms prickled with goose pimples, the flesh pulling against the atrophying sinew connecting it to her body.

She opened and closed her mouth, unable to form clear enough thoughts to realize she was thirsty. Dry and cracking skin broke her lips, the flesh around her mouth discolored and sore. One of the many enigmas about this disease was that the patients seemed to be dying of dehydration even as their bodies oozed fluids without restraint.

The light behind Amina's eyelids dimmed, allowing her a momentary reprieve. Sighing, she lifted a hand, cautiously this time, without knowing what she reached for. Pain and thirst twisted her mind, leaving her moaning and moving without direction.

"Amina?" A muted voice asked from across the room as light slashed through the darkness. Amina's body reacted to the light and she rolled to the side and pulled her head as far away from the invasion as possible.

"Amina?" it repeated, closing the door. The speaker seemed to expect some kind of reaction from the husk once named Amina. She moaned and gestured, her movements lacking all meaning, lolling her head toward the sound. A small movement compared to before. The brain learns quickly to minimize actions that cause pain.

The person spoke again. "Baby, are you in here?"

Amina's eyes burned, forcing her to close them. Thick mucus ran down her face, pooling in her ears where it blended with another, darker fluid that dripped from her inner ear. Tubes connected to her body, blood thinners and saline, plus other untested drugs that may or may not slow the progression of the disease. No one knew the final outcome.

Amina had been one of the first outside the large cities to become ill. Her work had taken her to New York City just before the CDC announced a spreading contagion and warned people to wear masks and gloves whenever in large crowds. In the beginning, when she sneezed, she attributed it to the usual spring cold. She didn't connect it with her trip or the increasing number of stories on the news about the burgeoning pandemic.

Now everyone she knew, everyone she had touched or stood next to on an elevator, had been exposed. By association, everyone they knew suffered. So far, little hope of a cure remained.

Rumors spread in Flushing, Queens, of a man who had made a complete recovery after receiving an antiviral medication for meningitis, but no one could verify or repeat the results. A hospital in Wichita claimed to have cured an ill child by introducing small amounts of mercury into her system. But the child soon died from the poison so many had hoped would cure her.

The light dimmed again and Amina sighed in relief. The stinging blue glow had been her constant companion. Now, without the initial intensity, Amina was learning to endure the pounding in her head. Thoughts tangled her mind, unable to congeal into coherent meaning beyond minimizing pain and seeking relief for the burning in her throat.

"*Fadlik*," Amina moaned, speaking in the mother tongue which she had not used in twenty years. "*Fadlik, Ummi...*"

"Amina, baby, I'm here..."

Eric Foxx rushed into the dark room containing his wife. She was one of three patients crammed into a small triage room. It should not have been used for admitted patients, but there was no where else for them to go. The hospital overflowed with the sick, both real and hypochondriacs who feared infection.

The number of infected had escalated and no one could get accurate information from the CDC anymore, if you reached them at all. Nine days had passed since the hospital admitted Amina and she barely received enough treatment to keep her alive. Or maybe she received all the treatment anyone could offer.

Eric had met his wife during the first Gulf War. She had been too young to realize that falling in love with a white American soldier would end any ties she had with her Kuwaiti family. Still, Amina had always been strong, stronger than any of the women he'd ever encountered. Strong enough to challenge his heart and mind and always win.

When they met, Eric had be twenty-three and Amina seventeen, too young for marriage by American standards, but with the consent of her mother, they wed in Kuwait and she came to America as his wife. The day after they left her home, she had received a call from her older brother. Her mother had been punished for going against their father's wishes by allowing Amina to wed an *alshit'an a'bi*. She died in a small medical clinic three days later.

Amina never again spoke Arabic or mentioned her family unless an unsuspecting acquaintance asked her about them. Few people asked a second time. Eric's wife had a quick and vicious sense of humor few wanted aimed at them. It was one of the things he loved most about her—she never ceased to surprise him with the way her mind worked; she was insightful and cutting.

Eric sped across the dim room, maneuvering around the cots and IV stands. He couldn't imagine how the nurses managed to get close enough to the patients to take care of them. Especially the guy in the middle. He was crammed in so tight no space existed between the cots. Between the overworked staff and overcrowded patients, conditions in the hospital plummeted. Soon, instead of being a safe haven from disease, it would become an incubator.

The room smelled of cleaning solution, sweat, and another, more primal and less recognizable scent. It singed the hairs in Eric's nose and made him breathe through his mouth.

At the foot of Amina's bed, Eric made out the shape of his wife and heard her soft moans. The light from the hall filtered in through Venetian blinds, providing the illusion of privacy in a public place.

"*Ummi*," she moaned, startling Eric.

"Mina, baby...I'm right here..." he took a step around the edge of her bed and flicked on the small florescent light above her.

Her screams began just a second before his. Agony echoed in her brain as the light pierced her eyelids, scorching her retinas and dissolving the thin membrane holding her eyes together. Then the viscous fluid that once filled her optic organs washed down her face, leaving behind only the hollowed out sockets.

The shocking torment reverberating within her skull dulled, and the blue light disappeared. Amina opened her lids, unaware she would not be able to see. She sat up, her body still resisting movement, but now something more important than pain held her attention.

Breathing in, she tasted something familiar in the air, something enticing that awoke an unexpected hunger. Her guts roiled and gurgled within, begging to be filled.

Eric's screams continued as he stared, mouth agape at the form that not a day ago had been his wife. His beautiful, exotic wife. Now before him sat something barely recognizable as human. Bits of her outer layers of skin peeled off, leaving her covered in raw red and fatty yellow chunks of flesh.

Beneath her skin had formed a transparent membrane, which held her organs and muscles in place. Her skin was sloughing away and being replaced with a substance more similar to the vitelline membrane that protects the yoke inside an egg.

Moisture was the single thing that would alleviate the intense pain of patients who progressed to this stage; morphine proved ineffective even in euthanizing dosages. Water wasn't enough. They tried emerging patients in tubs only to find the membrane would dissolve, leaving the patient exposed to the air and infection until a new layer grew back. Untreated, the patients oozed enough fluid from their orifices and through their remaining flesh to coat them with a slick slime. This appeared the sole thing to offer relief.

Amina tilted her head, searching for the enticing smell. The pain in her body decreased as her focus sharpened. As she moved, leaning toward whatever called to her with the power of a siren's song, her muscles and skin no longer tormented her.

Eric backed away from the creature before him, unable to reconcile the monstrous creature with the beautiful woman he had married. The black holes replacing her eyes gaped at him, sludge sliding down her olive skin, discolored with the tinge of death.

"Amina?" Eric asked, his back against the window, Venetian blinds bending and snapping out of place as he pushed as far away from her as possible.

A low growl came from her as she opened her mouth, almost like she was smiling at him, if not for the stench of sulfur emitting from her.

Eric inched toward the door, but each movement he made carried his scent through the air to the Amina-thing. Her tongue flicked out as if tasting him, and the empty orbs followed his movements. She growled again, a low predatory sound, before moving forward on the bed on all fours.

Naked and crouched like a wild animal, Amina allowed her instincts guide her. She couldn't see, but she didn't notice, instead perceiving her surroundings in sharp, clear contrast. The smells were distinct: two bodies registered as familiar, like brethren, and a third, enticing smell. The heat of Eric's body drew her in, and the scent of his skin called her. He spoke, making a sound she couldn't decipher, but the cadence appealed to her.

She rocked forward a bit, her need growing, creating a near-painful cramping in her body. Whatever gave off this smell was something she craved, something she needed. She needed it to survive, to exist. It had something she did not and without it she would cease to be. Biology demanded she act, that she consume and absorb this thing before her.

She sprang from her crouch. Eric fell beneath her, slipping away from her grasp. He screamed. To Amina's new form, the sounds meant nothing. The vibrations excited her, her body quivering with the anticipation of something she could not name.

Eric shrieked as the distorted face of his wife sniffed at him. She held him down with a strength she'd never possessed and should not have after so debilitating an illness. When she inhaled against his chest and moaned, Eric's cries became frantic.

The hallway outside of Amina's room was empty; the shift changing, the nurses exhausted and understaffed. Orderlies and technicians kept things running as best they could, but the small triage room down one hall of the ER had been forgotten in the chaos. No one heard Eric's wails except for the patients in adjacent rooms, too possessed with their own pain to register the sound as external.

A bloodcurdling howl ripped through the hospital as Amina consumed the source of her attraction. She crawled out of the room, still naked and on all fours. Eric's claret blood covered her, the arterial spray coating her face and torso. She stalked down the hall, looking for another victim, someone other than her brethren who might have the same intoxicating smell. Addicted, her need overwhelmed any remaining self Amina might have retained.

The triage room door closed, leaving Eric's lifeless body on the floor in the dark antechamber. His blood pooled around him, sections of skull and gray matter lay like forgotten puzzle pieces.

In the middle bed, John Petersen sat up, inspired by the scent of nourishment. The pain in his body receded as his eyes throbbed. Desperation to relieve the pressure surged through his limbs. Pushing the heels of his hands against his face, the ocular membranes burst. Soon he crouched on all floors and began the search for something to relieve his hunger.

COMING SOON

CPSIA information can be obtained at www.ICGtesting.com
Printed in the USA
BVOW010942180412

287952BV00002B/1/P

9 780983 876908